Battle
on the Ice

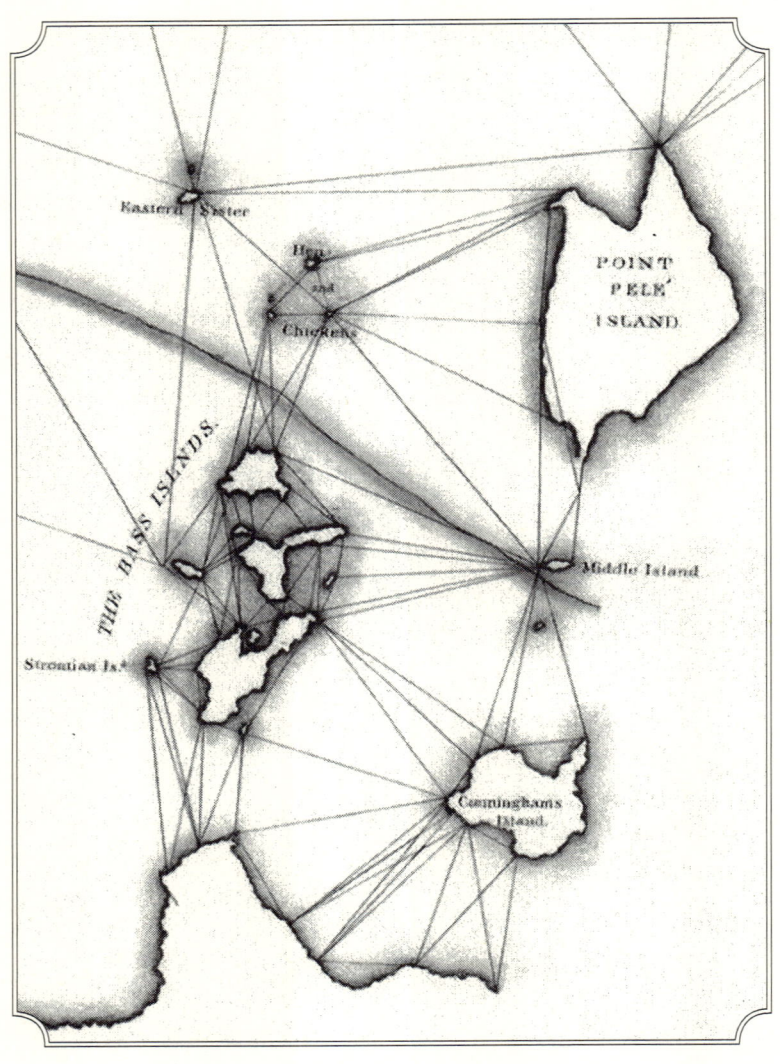

An 1843 printing of the
1820 Treaty of Ghent Survey Map

Battle on the Ice

JEAN RAE BAXTER

CROSSFIELD
PUBLISHING

CROSSFIELD PUBLISHING

www.crossfieldpublishing.com
books@crossfieldpublishing.com
2269 Road 120, R7, St. Marys, Ontario, N4X 1C9, Canada

Copyright © Jean Rae Baxter, 2023

ISBN: 978-1-990326-26-4 (Pbk.)
ISBN 978-1-990326-31-8 (ePub)

Printed and bound in Canada.

Cover art and design: Magdalene Carson RGD / New Leaf Publication Design

Library and Archives Canada Cataloguing in Publication

Title: Battle on the ice / Jean Rae Baxter.
Names: Baxter, Jean Rae, author.
Identifiers: Canadiana (print) 20230221688 | Canadiana (ebook) 20230221718 |
    ISBN 9781990326264 (softcover) | ISBN 9781990326318 (EPUB)
Subjects: LCSH: Canada—History—1791-1841—Fiction. | LCGFT: Historical fiction.
Classification: LCC PS8603.A935 B38 2023 | DDC C813/.6—dc23

For
Ruth Hutchins Nicholson UE

Author's Note

In the 1830s, Upper Canada was stirring with the political unrest and demand for reform that started with the American and French Revolutions. Insurrection against injustice had forced future newspaper editor William Lyon Mackenzie to flee to this province from Scotland. But once arrived here, he found matters no better. Power in Upper Canada was firmly in the hands of an aristocratic class that would later be referred to as the Family Compact. They detested democracy, believing that they were better able to maintain prosperity than any government elected by the ignorant masses. They believed that the natural order of society was hierarchical. These beliefs were opposed by protesters known as Reformers, who wanted popular election of those who wielded power, following an American model.

The Reformers had many American sympathizers ready to take up arms to support rebellion in Upper Canada. Although the United Stated had a Treaty of Neutrality with Great Britain, in 1838 Upper Canada was in a state of heightened tension as the threat of armed conflict rose. There were at least fourteen incursions into Canada. One of the most serious was the occupation of Pelee Island. There is no inhabited part of Canada that is further south.

On February 25 an armed force of about 300 men crossed the ice from Ohio and took over the undefended island. For five days they plundered and looted, until an army of Canadian militia and British regulars, led by Colonel John Maitland, arrived from Fort Malden (Amherstburg). On March 3 the invading army, defeated in one hour in a battle fought on the ice near the southwestern shore of the island, fled back to

Ohio in disarray, leaving Pelee Island to restore the tranquility it has enjoyed ever since.

Within the next three years, the power of the Family Compact was broken and in Canada the progress toward democracy began.

Battle on the Ice

CHAPTER ONE

In 1837 the fall harvest failed. To make our food last, we were eating just two meals a day. On these short rations we were always hungry. Pa whipped Susan for sneaking into the shed to eat seed potatoes. He said we had barely enough for next year's planting, without her stealing. Pa was right. But he shouldn't have whipped Susan. She's only five years old.

Just before Christmas, our horse died. Pa went out to the barn to feed him and found him dead in his stall. Prince was a sway-backed old nag, just a bag of bones. But he could still pull the plough. Without a horse, there'd be no planting in the spring. Pa was so downhearted that he left Prince lying there on the straw for a week. Finally Ma said, "He can't stay there all winter, even if the weather is cold."

So Pa and I got some harness on Prince and pulled him out of the stall. We hauled him head first out of the barn, his legs sticking into the air. It was hard work dragging an eight-hundred-pound dead horse over the snow-covered fields all the way to the woods at the back. That's where we left him. As we took the harness off him, Pa said, "There'll be nothing but bones left there in the spring."

It was during our walk back to the house that I made up my mind to leave home. A boy of fourteen can find work. There'd be more food for the others if I left. If I worked really hard, I could earn enough money buy us a new horse. Fifty dollars could get us a plug good enough to pull the plough. For one hundred dollars we could buy a really fine horse fit to pull a buggy in summer or a sleigh in winter.

I worried that Ma and Pa would say I was too young to go away on my own. If they said that, I'd tell them plenty of boys my age were already doing a man's work, and so could I. I had a dozen arguments all ready to convince them. So that evening, after we finished supper, I waited until Susan was excused from the table and was sitting on the settee playing with her doll. Then I rose from my chair, straightened my shoulders and said in a big voice, "Ma and Pa, I got something to tell you."

They were still sitting at the table. Ma hadn't yet cleared the plates. They both looked up. Neither said a word while I spoke. When I finished, they exchanged glances, looking embarrassed as if they'd already discussed that very thing and were taken aback because I said it first. Pa cleared his throat. "Dory, your mother and I are thankful you've saved us the pain of telling you that you have to leave. Unless we have a horse, this farm is finished. We have no money. We don't even have enough food to feed the four of us all winter long."

Ma said, "Dory, you're our only hope to keep the farm." Then she got up to clear the table.

There was a long silence while Pa sat with his elbow on the table and his chin propped on his hand. Then he said, "Son, there's no work to be had around here. Your best chance is to try one of those settlements along the north shore of Lake Erie. Colonel Talbot has settled thirty thousand people along that road. But stay away from border towns. Wherever there's Patriots meeting in their so-called Hunters' Lodges, there's going to be trouble." That was all the advice Pa had for me.

The next morning Ma packed a bundle for me to carry on a stick over my shoulder. In it she put my small clothes, my Sunday shirt, an extra pair of stockings, and a brush and comb. "You must keep yourself neat," she told me, "if you want anybody to hire you." She wrapped in a paper the slice of ham and piece of bread that would have been my supper.

As I hoisted my bundle over my shoulder and approached the door, Ma's lips trembled, but she did not shed a tear. I was the closer to weeping, because when Susan lifted her sweet little face toward mine and hugged my knees, my heart strings cracked to see how pale and thin she was.

"God go with you, son," said Ma. "Whatever hardships you face, you know to do the right thing."

"Yes, Ma," I said. "You and Pa taught me that."

Pa shook my hand. I noticed how his cheeks were dark with stubble. In better times, he had shaved every day; but for the week since old Prince died, he had been too discouraged to bother.

After I'd pried Susan's arms from around my knees and kissed the top of her head, I opened the door. A gust of snow blew in, so I stepped outside and closed the door behind me as fast as I could so the cabin wouldn't lose its warmth. I took a few steps, stopped, turned around, and saw all their faces at the window. Ma had her hand raised in a tiny wave good-bye.

Our land was on the heights above Queenston. It was the land the British Government gave my grandfather in 1785. That was after the war, when the Thirteen Colonies became the United States. All the Loyalists got land grants to thank them for staying true to King George.

As I walked down the lane, I passed our family burial plot, where four wooden crosses stood half buried in the snow. These marked the graves of Pa's parents and my two little brothers, Andrew and Alexander, who both died of diphtheria the year before Susan was born.

On reaching the road, I turned south. This road runs along the bank of the Niagara River all the way to Fort Erie. Before the Welland Canal was built to bypass Niagara Falls, ships coming up the river from Lake Ontario had to be unloaded at Queenston. Then their cargo was taken in wagons along this road to Fort Erie, where it was loaded onto other ships to be carried to settlements on the north shore of Lake Erie and even as far away as Detroit.

I was little more than a baby when the Welland Canal opened, so I never saw this. As far back as I remember, teams of oxen have hauled ships the whole twenty-seven miles through the canal. But the road is still busy, with the stagecoach using it, and farmers taking produce to market, and people on foot or on horseback going from place to place.

It was early in the day when I started out. I figured I could be in Fort Erie by late afternoon. The snow was falling steadily. As I walked, I tightened my shoulders against the cold to keep the heat in my body from escaping. My clothes were warm enough: woollen trousers and coat, linsey-woolsey shirt, square-toed boots with knitted stockings, a long bright red scarf around my neck, and on my head a coonskin hat. I ate my bread and ham as I walked.

Before long the snow was falling faster and faster, slowing my steps. The daylight was fading by the time I'd reached Chippawa, two miles above the Falls. Chippawa is a village on the Canadian side of the Niagara River. It faces Navy Island, which sits in the middle of the river.

Navy Island belongs to Canada. The boundary between Canada and the United States runs along the middle of the channel on the far side of Navy Island. Facing Navy Island from the American side of the river is Fort Schlosser.

Just before Chippawa, I passed a fortification manned by our soldiers, by which I mean British and Canadian soldiers. It wasn't much of a fortification—just logs and one cannon mounted on a carriage. The soldiers had their cannon pointed at Navy Island. Through the falling snow I saw about twenty redcoats. If they even saw me, they paid me no attention as I walked by.

Chippawa was one of those border towns Pa warned me against. I didn't plan to stay there to look for work. But somebody in Chippawa was sure to need wood chopped or a stable cleaned. I decided to stop there for the night. When the weather cleared, I'd continue on my way to Fort Erie. I reckoned the tavern in Chippawa would be the best place to find food and lodging. So when I reached the tavern, I stamped the snow from my boots on the porch floor, opened the door and walked right in.

CHAPTER TWO

The tavern's public room was welcoming and warm, with a good fire blazing in the stone fireplace. On the mantel, wax candles burned brightly. The room was furnished with benches, tables and chairs.

Two men of middle age were sitting by the fire smoking their pipes. They looked up at me as I pulled off my coonskin hat. One rose from his chair. He was a short, stubby man, his complexion reddish, his chin double and his body plump. He regarded me from under bushy eyebrows with a pair of shrewd grey eyes.

"Welcome, traveller. You do well to come out of the cold and seek lodging here."

Taking him for the tavern owner, I said, "Sir, I have no money to pay for a room, but I'll gladly work for a night's lodging." He didn't look like the sort of man who would thrust a poor boy out of doors to freeze in the snow. So I stood holding my coonskin hat in one hand, for my other hand still supported the stick with my bundle over my shoulder.

"Runaway, are you?"

"No, sir! I left home to look for work to help my family."

"So you need more than just a place to sleep." His expression became stern, but not unkind. "Can you split a log? Can you chop kindling?"

"Yes, sir. Yes, sir."

"Then I can use you. My last boy ran off two days ago to join Mackenzie's militia on Navy Island. He left me high and dry."

"Sir, I would never do that!" I spoke firmly, though I had no idea what Mackenzie's militia might be. I felt a tingle of excitement inside. The tavern owner was going to hire me! Just like that! I scarcely believed my good fortune. Even though Pa had warned me to stay away from border towns like Chippawa, I was overjoyed to realize that I need go no further to find work.

"Sam Kemp's my name," he said.

"I'm Theodore Dickson. Everybody calls me Dory."

Mr. Kemp turned to the other man, who sat smoking quietly while we talked. "I'll be back in a minute." Then he spoke again to me. "The way it's snowing, there's sure to be other travellers who'll find they can go no further today. When they come in out of the cold, they need a blazing fire to welcome them. My tavern has ten guest rooms, and every room has a fireplace or an iron stove to heat it. There's also a cook stove in the kitchen. All these stoves and fireplaces take a ton of wood to keep them burning." He paused. "You'll have other tasks, but your main work will be to split logs and chop kindling."

"Yes, sir. I can do that." I looked at the meager pile of logs stacked against the wall beside the fireplace. Barely enough to last the rest of the day. "I'll get right to work, Mr. Kemp."

"Well, Dory, if you're willing to work for food, a bed and two dollars a week, I'll show you to your room."

Mr. Kemp led me through a low doorway into a hallway with rooms on both sides. Halfway down the hall, he opened the door to a windowless chamber not much bigger than a broom closet. There was no stove or fireplace to heat it. The only furniture was a narrow cot, with a grey blanket on top and a wooden box at the foot.

"This is your room," he said, "as long as I don't need it for a paying guest. In that case, you can sleep on a bench in the kitchen until this room is free again."

"Thank you, sir." I entered the room and laid my bundle on the cot.

Mr. Kemp remained standing in the doorway. "You can start work as soon as you've had a bite to eat. The woodshed is behind the main building." Then he paused and looked me straight in the eye. "First, there's one thing I must make clear. There's a lot of trouble along the border, but I don't take sides. You can't either if you're going to work for me."

"My father told me there was trouble on the border," I said. "At home, we didn't talk about politics. We didn't take sides."

"Keep it that way. My tavern is neutral ground. There are gentlemen on both sides who feel comfortable gathering here. This is a place where friends can meet to share a pint. Colonel McNab dropped by yesterday to enjoy a glass of punch by the fire in the public room. He has his headquarters in Chippawa."

"Who's Colonel McNab?" I asked.

"Allan McNab is the officer in charge of the troops the government sent here to keep an eye on the Patriots over on Navy Island. He had Commodore Drew of the Royal Marines with him. These are important men." Mr. Kemp paused. "Under this roof, visitors are courteous to one another whatever their politics. My business depends upon keeping it that way. I'm a tavern keeper, not a politician. I don't want this place to become a battlefield, like Montgomery's Tavern in Toronto. That affair ended with one man dead and the tavern burned to the ground."

This was the first time I'd heard of Montgomery's Tavern. It would not be the last. As soon as Mr. Kemp left, I unpacked my bundle, stowing my spare clothes in the box at the foot of the bed. Then I found my way to the kitchen and introduced myself to the cook. She was a big, soft-looking woman, the complete opposite of my mother. The cook told me her name was Nancy. She gave me a roast beef sandwich, a bowl of pea soup and a cup of tea. As I ate, I thought about my parents and little Susan, and I wished that I could share this good food with them.

After I had eaten, I went out to the shed to chop wood. I split logs until the light failed and my arms and shoulders ached. Then I returned to the kitchen to ask Nancy for a candle. She gave me a stub long enough to last until I went to bed. By its light I made my way to my little room, where I set the candlestick on the box at the foot of my bed.

My bed was just a narrow platform of bare boards with a straw mattress that bore the impress of the last person who had slept there. The mattress needed a good shaking. Otherwise, it would be nearly as uncomfortable to sleep on as the bare boards. So I picked up one end and lifted it off the bed, and then . . . and then . . . I saw a folded paper squeezed between two of the bed boards. I set down the mattress, pulled out the paper and unfolded it. My heart nearly stopped, for in my hands I held a fifty-dollar banknote, "payable to bearer", drawn on the Bank of Upper Canada.

I started to shake. What if somebody saw me with the banknote and thought I had stolen it? I must give it to Mr. Kemp right now. That was the only thought in my mind. With the banknote in my pocket and the candle in my hand, I hurried to the public room.

Mr. Kemp was still there, saying goodnight to the man he had been talking with beside the fire. I stayed back in the shadows until Mr. Kemp was alone. When he saw me there, holding the candle, he said, "What's wrong, Dory? You look like you've seen a ghost."

I pulled the banknote from my pocket. "Sir, I found this under the mattress."

He took it from my hand, and as he read it, his bushy eyebrows rose. "Well! I know where this came from!" Mr. Kemp looked straight into my eyes. "Dory, you have done more good than you will ever know. The return of this banknote will save the reputation of a decent man—falsely suspected of stealing it. I'll look after the matter and see that his name is cleared, but I may not tell you more."

Of course, I was curious to hear the story. But it was not mine to know. I went back to my room, where I had just enough time to shake the mattress before my candle guttered out. As I lay awake waiting for sleep to come, I thought about the banknote. Fifty dollars would buy a good-enough horse to pull our plough. I wished that the banknote had been mine.

CHAPTER THREE

The next afternoon the stagecoach arrived, carrying six passengers inside, and the half-frozen driver outside on the box. The snow had changed from fluffy flakes to hard grains of ice, with which the wind lashed my face as I rushed into the yard to help the passengers from the coach. There were four gentlemen, a lady and the lady's maid. The lady wore a red velvet cape trimmed with black fur. Her maid's cape was brown and plain, but looked just as warm as that of her mistress. The gentlemen carried portmanteaux and wore heavy overcoats. After the passengers had hurried inside, I helped the driver stable the horses and give them a good rubdown. I suspected that the driver would be given my little room to sleep in, which was exactly what happened.

The tavern was full of guests that night, every room occupied. The lady and her maid dined in their room; it was upstairs, so I didn't see much of them. The public room was thronged with men, those who had arrived on the stagecoach as well as other guests. They ate a splendid dinner, drank punch, smoked their pipes, talked and laughed. They didn't discuss politics. At all times they were courteous to one another, just as Mr. Kemp said they would be.

After dinner, Mr. Kemp sent me to the kitchen to help Nancy scour the pots and pans. When that was done, Nancy and I feasted upon the remains of the dinner that had been served to the guests. I ate three slabs of roast pork, mopping up the gravy with crusty white bread. Nancy laughed to see the pleasure I took in food. It was almost midnight by the time we finished.

She went off to her own room, and I lay down on the wooden bench that stood against the wall opposite the fireplace. She had given me a pillow and a blanket. Despite the hardness of the bench, I went right to sleep.

Men's voices woke me in the middle of the night. Opening my eyes, I saw a man bending over the fireplace grate, lighting a twist of paper from an ember. Candles flared, and I realized that there were eight or ten men in the kitchen.

"What!" I exclaimed, sitting bolt upright.

They turned as one and stared at me, looking surprised and displeased. It was obvious that they had not noticed me in the near darkness, lying on the bench. I recognized some of them as guests at the tavern; they had been among those eating, drinking, smoking and talking in the public room. The others must have just arrived, their cloaks and overcoats dusted with snow.

They glared at me. There was only one who gave me a friendly look. He was a sturdy fellow with sandy hair, red whiskers and sharp blue eyes. "Laddie," he said with a Scottish burr, "We didn't expect to find somebody sleeping in the kitchen. We're here for a private meeting of the Hunters' Lodge. Does that name mean anything to you?"

"No, sir. I've heard the name, but I don't know anything about it." This answer was not completely true, because Pa had mentioned trouble brewing wherever Patriots met in their Hunters' Lodges.

He looked disappointed with my answer. "We're a society dedicated to the fight for equality."

"Who're you fighting?"

"Have you heard of the Family Compact?"

"Yes. My father told me about them. He says the Family Compact is a bunch of rich families who hog all the money and power for themselves."

"Ay, that's the truth! It sounds like your father supports the Patriots."

"No, sir. My father doesn't support either side. He says the

Family Compact run Upper Canada, but even if they lost power, nothing would change for poor people like us."

The man frowned. "Do you know why he says that?"

"He says it wasn't the Family Compact that caused the cold and rain last spring that made our corn rot in the ground before it sprouted. It wasn't the Family Compact that made our cow eat mouldy sweet clover so she died. It was diphtheria, not the Family Compact that killed my little brothers. And it was old age that killed our horse."

The man shook his head. "Laddie, I'm sorry for your family's misfortune. There are some things no government can change. But government by the people will serve all the people, not just a rich upper class, and that will spread prosperity all around."

"Come on, Duncan!" a man in an overcoat muttered loudly. "Tell the boy to go about his business. We have work to do."

I was glad to leave them. According to Pa, these so-called Patriots are the fellows causing all the trouble along the border. Yet the man called Duncan did not seem dangerous. He looked at me kindly.

"Laddie, you and I can talk about this some other time. Right now, I must ask you to leave us."

I stood up and reached for my bundle, which I had repacked when the stagecoach driver took over my little chamber. I thought I might go to the public room to sleep on a chair. I didn't care where I slept, and I was so groggy with fatigue that I could have gone to sleep standing there. Duncan must have seen this, for he said, "I have an idea. There's a trundle bed under the bed in my room. You can have it for the night."

"I'll be back in a minute," he said to the others. Then he turned to me. "My name's Duncan Fraser. What's yours?"

"Dory Dickson."

"Well, Dory, I can see you need a good night's rest. Come with me." He took a candle and led me down the passage to the room across the hall from the one that had been mine. He pulled out the trundle bed. I fell upon it and closed my eyes before Duncan even left the room.

CHAPTER FOUR

s soon as I opened my eyes in the morning, I rolled over
and looked out the window. Nothing but snow falling thick
and fast. They'll need wood for the fires, I thought. I jumped up
from the trundle bed, pulled on my clothes and tiptoed from
the room without waking Duncan, who was snoring peacefully.

By the time I had carried in half a dozen armfuls of firewood,
Nancy had a bowl of oatmeal porridge ready for me. At my
place was a tumbler full of milk. I hadn't had a glass of milk
since our cow died months ago. Eagerly I raised the glass to
my lips. But then I thought of Susan, and I saw my little sister's thin, tiny fingers lifting the glass and her wide blue eyes
peering over the rim. I had a lump in my throat as I swallowed
the milk. With all my heart, I wished that it had been for her.

After I had eaten and tended the fires in the guest rooms,
I asked Mr. Kemp for permission to go for a walk. He looked
surprised that I wanted to venture out in the snow, but he
said that I might. Although it wasn't a pleasant day for a walk,
I was curious to have a better look at the fortification that I'd
seen the day before.

Even though it was late December, the Niagara River was
still open. When I reached the fortification, the redcoats were
on duty, trying to watch what was happening over on Navy
Island. They had a cannon mounted on a carriage. I would have
liked to see some action, but with the snow falling so heavily, I
figured there was little chance of anything exciting happening
that day. No point wasting ammunition if you can't see your
target through the snow.

I asked one of the redcoats, "What's going on over there?"

"Don't you know?" He laughed. "The Patriots are raising an army. They have four hundred men on Navy Island, drilling to invade the mainland. Navy Island is the capital of the Republic of Canada."

"There is no Republic of Canada," I protested. "We're a monarchy. Victoria is our queen."

"Not according to William Lyon Mackenzie. He has declared himself Chief of the Executive Committee of the Provisional Government of Canada. If you join the Patriots' army, they'll give you three hundred acres of land and one hundred dollars in silver."

"One hundred dollars!" I gave a whistle. I didn't care about the land, but one hundred dollars was enough to buy a good horse and still have some money left over.

"Yes." The soldier laughed again. "It's payable at Toronto in May—after the Patriots liberate Canada and throw out the Family Compact."

His words were a jolt of reality. Before I could collect my hundred dollars in silver, the Patriots would have to defeat a whole army of well-trained government soldiers. Not much chance of that!

I was about to tell the redcoat that I had no quarrel with either side, when an officer on horseback arrived at the fortification, his approach silent and barely visible through the thick-falling snow. He was mounted on a fine-looking chestnut horse. The soldier who had been chatting with me touched his hat to him and addressed him as Colonel McNab. There was some discussion, which soon ended. I heard Colonel McNab say that he was on his way to his headquarters. The redcoat saluted the colonel, who then rode off in the direction of Chippawa.

I returned to the tavern and to my work. By nightfall I had half a cord stacked against the fireplace wall in the public room. But my tasks weren't finished yet. With so many guests to feed, Mr. Kemp sent me to the kitchen to help Nancy. I was taking platters of food to the public room and carrying back dirty dishes right up to eleven o'clock. Then there were dishes to wash and pots and pans to scrub. It was midnight before everything was done to Nancy's satisfaction.

By this time, the bench that stood against the kitchen wall was looking mighty comfortable. Nancy brought me a blanket and pillow, as she had done the night before. My bundle was still in Duncan's room. *Maybe he hasn't gone to bed yet,* I thought. Duncan had been in the public room talking with other guests all evening. So he might still be up. I wanted my bundle. I asked Nancy for a candle. She gave me a stub to light my way.

Sure enough, Duncan's door was wide open. He was sitting in an armchair by the fire reading a newspaper. The banner across the top gave its name: *The Constitution.*

"Hello!" I greeted him. "I've come to pick up my bundle. I'll be sleeping in the kitchen tonight, unless the Hunters' Lodge is meeting there again."

"No chance of that. They won't meet again for at least a month." He paused. "I was hoping you'd come by to get your bundle. I want to tell you a few things about the Family Compact and why we're fighting to destroy its power." He pointed to a chair on the other side of the fireplace. "Take a seat."

I was tired, and I didn't want to hear about the Family Compact right now. But I didn't wish to seem ungrateful for Duncan's kindness in letting me sleep in his room the previous night. So I placed my candlestick on a table, sat down and prepared to listen.

"There are people who believe that democracy is dangerous," he began, "and that power should remain in the hands of a ruling class."

I yawned. Seeing this, he frowned. "Dory, pay attention! These people, the Family Compact, control everything in Upper Canada. Not just the government. They also run the church and the law courts. They really are one big family, because they intermarry so that the strands are twisted together. Brothers, sons, uncles, nephews—all have their fingers in the pot. This situation would be bad even if they gave us good government. But they don't. They're greedy, incompetent and corrupt."

His voice grew louder and louder, as if he were giving a speech to a big crowd and not just to one boy who might be too sleepy to pay attention. He continued. "That's why simple farmers and shopkeepers are ready to take up arms. We must seize power from the Family Compact and give it to the common people!"

He stopped talking, and while he caught his breath, he looked keenly at me, likely wondering whether I was still awake.

"What you're saying makes sense," I said, to show him that I was paying attention, "But I can't take sides . . . not if I want to work for Mr. Kemp. He's made that clear."

"Of course he has." Duncan smiled, his voice much calmer now. "It's late. I won't keep you any longer."

I rose from the chair and was about to pick up my bundle from the floor where it lay, when suddenly a light appeared outside the window, a rosy pink glow, brighter than sunrise. Duncan sprang up. He ran to the window and looked out.

"What the Deuce! It's a ship on fire!"

I raced to the window. The snow had stopped, and I could see everything clearly. It was indeed a ship on fire, drifting down the Niagara River. Flames leaping sky high.

"It's the *Caroline*," said Duncan. "I wondered what that Royal Navy officer was doing here with Sheriff Hamilton, Deputy Sheriff Alexander McLeod and Colonel McNab. They must have dispatched men in boats to cut her loose from her wharf at Fort Schlosser and set her on fire. Fort Schlosser is on American soil, so that's an act of war!"

I could not tear my eyes away from the spectacle. I'd once seen a barn go up in flames; it was like that. But this was even more terrific, because the flames from the burning ship didn't just light up the sky, their reflection made the water seem to burn. The ship looked as if she might blaze all the way to Niagara Falls two miles downriver. But while she was still in sight, the *Caroline* stopped moving.

"Ha!" said Duncan. "She's stranded in a bed of bulrushes."

There she sat, still burning, although as the minutes passed the flames no longer rose as high. "What kind of ship is she?" I asked.

"She's a forty-six-ton steamer owned by a man in Buffalo. The Patriots have been using her to carry recruits and weapons from Fort Schlosser over to Navy Island. That's where William Lyon Mackenzie is training his army to invade Canada. Four hundred men! Some are Canadians, but most are freedom-loving Americans who want Canadians to have the kind of liberty that they enjoy."

I thought about this. The Americans were our neighbours, but I didn't think of them as friends. My mother was just a little girl when the American army burned Niagara. They did it at night in the middle of winter, so people were left freezing in the snow. Knowing Ma's story, I couldn't believe any Americans really cared about Canadians. Maybe Duncan didn't know about that war we had with the United States. He was from Scotland. His history was different from ours in Upper Canada.

"This will change everything," Duncan said quietly, "though I'm not sure exactly how."

We heard noises in the hall. People were shouting and running back and forth. "I want to see what's going on," I said.

"Go ahead. But close my door when you leave. It will be safer for me to keep out of the way until this settles down."

I took my candle and left his room, shutting the door behind me. There was a commotion in the hall, men bumping into each other in the dark. Forgetting about my bundle, I headed for the public room, not for the kitchen. There would be no sleep that night.

CHAPTER FIVE

Duncan Fraser and I weren't the only ones who saw the *Caroline* on fire. Most of the tavern's guest rooms overlooked the river, their windows giving a clear view all the way to the bed of reeds where the blazing ship lay stranded. Some witnesses still hadn't gone to bed when the *Caroline* drifted by. Others had been awakened by the light of her flames. An excited crowd now gathered in the public room to talk about it. "Like a blazing meteor," everyone agreed. Yet not everyone was thrilled by the spectacle. Some worried about consequences. Like Duncan, they said it was an act of war for a Canadian armed force to cut loose and burn a ship moored on the United States side of the river. What if President Van Buren sent troops to the frontier?

I listened as I built up the fire in the fireplace and stoked the stove. I couldn't have told which speakers were sympathetic to the Patriots or which supported the Family Compact, for all were united in their fear of war. One of the men, a dignified gentleman who had arrived on the stagecoach, assured Mr. Kemp that President Van Buren was opposed to war. "I hope you're right," Mr. Kemp answered. "I don't want an American army sitting on our doorstep. Tavern owners don't make money out of war."

The excitement died down, but not the conversation. Every seat in the public room was taken, and it seemed that each man had a different bit of information to contribute. One gentleman, richly robed in a red silk dressing gown with black velvet lapels, announced that he had had a premonition of something like this.

"A couple of days ago, when I came into the public room to read the newspaper, I saw Colonel McNab talking with Commodore Andrew Drew of the Royal Navy. They had their heads together. They glanced over at me; then they left the room. One hour later, when I happened to look out the window, I saw Commodore Drew and our Deputy Sheriff Alexander McLeod in a boat being rowed upriver toward the head of Navy Island. 'Something's afoot,' I said to myself."

"They must have been reconnoitering," said a man with rumpled hair, whose unbuttoned overcoat did not quite cover his long white nightshirt. "At eleven o'clock this evening—I happened to check my watch before blowing out my candle to go to bed, so I know the exact time—I looked out my window. What I saw were seven open boats setting out from Chippawa, heading toward the American side of the river. Eight or nine men in each boat. They kept upstream from Navy Island. No doubt about it. They were on their way to Fort Schlosser."

Mr. Kemp frowned. "That's about fifty men—a considerable armed force. It sounds like they planned to board the ship, not just cut her loose. If there was bloodshed, the Americans will retaliate. It might lead to war."

By this time the sky was turning grey, although the sun had not yet risen. The men who had arrived on the stagecoach returned to their rooms to dress and pack their portmanteaux. Soon the lady and her maid appeared, the maid struggling with suitcases and hat boxes. By the time all six passengers had reassembled in the public room, the tavern's other guests had left, probably going back to their beds to catch up on their sleep. Now that my little room was free, that was what I wanted to do. But Mr. Kemp sent me outdoors to help the stagecoach driver harness the horses.

As the driver and I tightened the traces, he told me that this would be his last trip for the season. "Look at that snow!

It's halfway up to the wheel hubs. If we run into a snow drift, we're stuck." He shook his head, "From Chippawa to Niagara-on-the Lake is only eleven miles, but we'll be hard pressed to make it in one day."

A few minutes later, his passengers emerged from the tavern and took their places in the coach. The driver climbed up to his seat on the box and cracked his whip. The horses strained in their harness to get the stagecoach moving, but they were well rested. In a few moments they had it going. As the coach rolled away, its wheels made dark furrows in the new-fallen snow.

When I went back indoors, Mr. Kemp was waiting for me. He was standing just inside the door, rubbing his hands together nervously. He gave me a tense smile. "Dory, I'm going to need some special help from you. Take yourself to the kitchen for breakfast. Then I'll tell you about it." I wondered what task he had in mind. What special help could he want from me?

Nancy had provided the stagecoach passengers with a cold breakfast of bread and cheese before they left. Now she had the cook-stove fired up and a big pot of porridge ready for the staff. A man and two girls were already seated at the long wooden table. So far, Nancy was the only fellow worker I'd had a chance to meet. I sat down with the man and the girls. Nancy filled my bowl with porridge, and I topped it with a sprinkle of maple sugar.

The others introduced themselves. The man, Howard, smelled of the stable. He told me that he looked after Mr. Kemp's horses. The girls were young and pretty. They wore white aprons over striped blue and white dresses, and ruffled white caps on their heads. They said they cleaned the guestrooms. The girls told me about the boy whose place I had taken after he left to join the Patriot army on Navy Island. "He was a wild boy," one told me.

The other girl giggled. "If he ever collects the hundred dollars that Mackenzie promised, he'll have it spent in a week."

Howard, who had the steady voice of a man good with horses, chuckled, "That's a big 'if'. Think what it would cost! They say Mackenzie has four hundred recruits on Navy Island. That makes it forty thousand dollars he'd have to pay. Where could he get that much money?" Howard paused. "But that's not a serious question, because Mackenzie won't have any more success invading Canada than he did starting a revolution in Toronto."

"A revolution in Toronto!" This was news to me.

"Three weeks ago, at a place called Montgomery's Tavern."

"I've heard about Montgomery's Tavern. Mr. Kemp told me a man was killed in the battle, and the tavern burned to the ground."

"It wasn't much of a battle," said Howard. "Mackenzie's officers didn't know how to lead and his men didn't know how to fight. As soon as the regular army arrived, they scattered in every direction. To make his escape, Mackenzie had to swim across a river full of floating ice."

"In December!"

"It was either swim for his life or be hanged for treason if Colonel McNab's soldiers captured him." Howard pushed his chair back from the table. "It's time for me to get back to work." As he stood up, he said, "William Lyon Mackenzie is either a maniac or the greatest man in Upper Canada. So far, I can't decide."

Howard's place at the table was taken by a broad-shouldered man who mumbled that he'd been up since daybreak loading a sled. I didn't want to keep Mr. Kemp waiting, so I said goodbye and left the kitchen just after the newcomer sat down.

When I returned to the public room, Mr. Kemp was alone. He motioned me to take a chair at one of the tables, and he sat down across from me. Looking at me solemnly from under his bushy eyebrows, he said, "Can you handle a horse and sled?"

"Yes, sir."

"Good." He cleared his throat. "My dear wife passed away last summer."

I was speechless. Why was he telling me this? I didn't know what to say. At last I managed to mumble "Sir, I'm sorry." I could see that Mr. Kemp's announcement was leading up to something, but I had no idea what.

"It was a great loss." Again he cleared his throat. "Here's the situation. My wife owned a spinning wheel and a loom that were her prized possessions. When she realized that she was soon to meet her Maker, she made me promise to give them to her best friend. Her name is Elizabeth Fox. Mrs. Fox and her husband Jacob live in Gosfield Township near Albertville on the north shore of Lake Erie. Colonel Talbot's road goes right by their farm. The problem is, parts of the Talbot Road are corduroy—made of logs—the very devil for horses' hooves and wagon wheels. That's why I waited for a good snowfall before making arrangements to send the spinning wheel and loom to Mrs. Fox. It's easier to transport goods by sled than by wagon.

"Naturally, I'd prefer to deliver my wife's bequest in person, but my business running the tavern keeps me here."

I saw where this talk was leading, and my heart sank. I'd never been more than ten miles from home in my whole life. "Sir," I said, "Are you asking *me* to do this? It's a long way. I'm just fourteen years old. Besides that, you hardly know me."

"Dory, I'm an expert judge of character. Through my life I've often had to make decisions based on a first impression. Yours was a good one. And when you gave me that banknote you had found under the mattress, I knew I could trust you completely." He slid me a cunning look, as if we were conspirators. "Gosfield is two hundred miles from Chippawa. To you that may sound like the other side of the world. But you can make the journey one step at a time. There are settlements all along the Talbot Road. I have many friends in that part of the country, as well as men who owe me a favour. I'll write you a letter of introduction to people who'll make you welcome." He paused. "Let me see. Tonight you'll stay at the home of Leonard Goodwin in Fort Erie. Tomorrow night you'll rest at a little place called Anthony's Mills at the mouth of the Grand River. Don't worry. I'll give you a complete list of names and places. You'll lodge at farms and in towns. Tillsonburg. St. Thomas. Morpeth." As he spoke, his reddish face became redder still and there were beads of sweat on his forehead. For my part, I shivered just thinking about such a journey.

I made one last attempt to change his mind. "Mr. Kemp, tomorrow is New Year's Eve. The tavern will be full of guests. You need me to chop wood for the fireplaces and stoves."

He didn't seem to hear me. "I'll provide you with cash to meet any expenses that crop up." He rose to his feet. "It's only seventeen miles to Fort Erie. The sled is already loaded. I'll tell Howard to harness a strong, steady horse to pull it." He looked at the clock that stood on the mantelpiece. The time was ten o'clock. "In two hours I'll have the letter written and a list of names and places ready for you. You've been up all night. Use the time to get some sleep."

He left me still sitting, stunned at the thought of what lay ahead. But if I wanted to keep working for Mr. Kemp, I had to follow orders. Two dollars a week was good pay.

CHAPTER SIX

ow that the stagecoach had left, my tiny windowless chamber was mine again. As soon as I had closed the door, I pulled off my boots and collapsed onto the lumpy, straw-filled mattress and fell asleep. I might have stayed in that state all day, had a fist pounding on the door not wakened me. That fist belonged to one of the girls I had met at breakfast.

"Dory," she shouted through the door, "Mr. Kemp has everything ready for you. I'm to take you to his rooms."

"Just a minute," I grunted, easing myself off the mattress. Still groggy, I ran my fingers through my messy hair and pulled on my boots.

Leaving my chamber, I followed her to the public room and then down a short hall to Mr. Kemp's private quarters. At her knock, Mr. Kemp opened the door, welcoming me to a pleasant office that was furnished with a sofa upholstered in dark red plush, a couple of chairs, and a desk with a cover made of narrow wooden slats fastened together. He rolled up the cover, revealing many little drawers and cubby-holes. From one of the cubby-holes Mr. Kemp took out an envelope. He gave it to me. It was unsealed. On the front of the envelope were the words, "To Whom It May Concern."

"This," he said, "is the letter of introduction for you to show my friends. They will provide lodging for you and stabling for the horse." Then he gave me ten dollars in bank notes, and finally he took from a drawer a list of names. He held the list out to me; but when I reached to take it, he drew back his hand. "Dory, this list must be a secret between you and me. Never

show it to anyone. If there's a chance of it falling into anyone's
hands but yours, you must burn it and crumble the ashes." He
looked hard into my eyes. "Do I have your promise to do this?"

After assuring him that no other eyes than mine would
ever see the list, I crossed my heart to show that my very soul
was security for this vow. My promise satisfied him, and he
gave me the list. There were a dozen names on it. Most had an
address or other direction to reach the person's home or place
of business. I folded the list and thrust it deep into my trousers' pocket When Mr. Kemp closed his desk, the cover rolled
down as smooth as water flowing over a dam. I'd never before
seen anything like that desk.

"One final warning," he said. "I've had the spinning wheel
and loom covered by a heavy tarpaulin tied down so that not
a flake of snow or drop of rain can get inside. Moisture would
ruin the wood. So be sure not to loosen the ropes or the bolts
in the sled floor. That's the only way to keep the cargo safe,
whatever the weather."

"I'll remember that," I said. "I'll keep it tight and dry all the
way to Jacob Fox's farm."

When I went to Duncan Fraser's room to pick up my bundle, I found Duncan standing in front of the looking glass over
his washstand, trimming his reddish whiskers with a pair of
scissors. I began at once to tell him about the journey that lay
ahead—the great distance I must travel alone through a part
of the country where I had never been before. While I talked,
he kept snipping away at his whiskers, paying more attention
to his reflection in the looking glass than to me. He snipped
a few hairs from the left side, then a few more from the right.
Not until he was satisfied did he lay down his scissors and
turn to me.

"Well, Laddie, Sam Kemp certainly hasn't wasted any time."

I thought I knew what Duncan meant about not wasting
any time, so I agreed. "He couldn't have sent the loom and
spinning wheel any sooner. He had to wait for a good snowfall before he could use the sled." I picked up my bundle from

the floor where I had left it and took out my comb. Duncan moved aside so that I could comb my hair at the washstand.

I dipped my comb in the water in his wash bowl and carefully parted my hair, which was brown and curly. I took a close look at my upper lip and chin to see if there might be a trace of whiskers. Nothing yet.

"You seem worried about this journey," Duncan said. "There's nothing to warry about."

"I'm not worried—at least not much. Mr. Kemp has given me a list of people who'll help me."

"I thought he would. Sam has plenty of connections. There'll be good lodging for you and stabling for the horse. As you say, you'll see a part of the country you've not seen before."

"Have you been there?" I asked as I retied my bundle.

"Laddie, I've been everywhere in Upper Canada and Lower Canada that Hunters' Lodges meet. In Lower Canada the lodges are called *les Frères Chasseurs*. In that province *Les Patriotes* are led by a great man named Louis-Joseph Papineau. I'm useful because I speak both French and English."

"I'm surprised you can speak French," I said. "You're from Scotland. How did you learn to speak French?"

"Ach! I left Scotland at age fifteen, when my uncle offered me a position at his business in Montreal. He had emigrated twenty years earlier and returned to Scotland for a family visit. My uncle was a successful merchant, and my parents considered this a great opportunity for me. But I was not a good hand at scratching in a ledger or counting change in a money box. After one year, I left Montreal and headed for the bush. Travelling about, trading with the Indians—that was the life for me. I became a *coureur de bois* and learned the language to go with it. After ten years, I happened to be in Quebec. There I heard Papineau give a speech. He spoke of freedom and liberty. This changed everything for me. At twenty-six, I found a cause to devote my life to.

"So I still travel about, though not in the bush. I organize Hunters' Lodges in the United States as well as in Upper and

Lower Canada. Mostly in border cities—Buffalo, Detroit—where hundreds of Americans want to help us throw off the yoke of British tyranny and turn Canada into a republic."

"Why do you want Canada to be a republic?"

"Because it's ridiculous for us to be ruled by a silly eighteen-year-old girl who's never been to Canada and whose only qualification is that she's the daughter of the fourth son of mad King George. I don't suppose she's even heard of the Family Compact, but she's part of the system. Look how it works here in Upper Canada. A dozen or so families have everything sewn up for their benefit—Government, Law Courts, Church. They stay on top by keeping everybody else down. Is that fair?"

"Not fair at all," I agreed. "Can't we rid ourselves of the Family Compact and keep the Queen?" The Family Compact sounded like a bunch of scoundrels, but I had nothing against Queen Victoria. Being young myself, I didn't think her age should be held against her. As for accepting help from Americans, I didn't trust them one bit. But this was no time to argue about Patriots and politics. I thanked Duncan for his kindness and told him that I must be on my way.

He slapped me on the back. "Safe journey!"

CHAPTER SEVEN

The glare of sunlight off the white snow dazzled my eyes. Blinking, I saw the sled waiting for me, already packed. It was like a wagon on iron runners. Nothing fancy. It had wood sides two feet high and a board for the driver's seat. About four feet wide by eight feet long, it was a good size for one horse to pull. A heavy tarpaulin, lashed down and securely tied to ring bolts in the floor, completely covered the load. I could see that the man who packed it had made sure neither wind nor snow could penetrate that cover.

I was inspecting the sled's runners when Howard came out from the stable leading a chunky, dark brown horse with a shiny, thick mane and tail. "This is Labelle," he said. "You're lucky to have her to pull your sled. Labelle is a Canadian horse. Do you know what that means?"

Well, of course I did! Whether it's under a saddle or pulling a load, there's nothing on four hooves to beat that breed. It's true that our horse Prince had been a common plug but, like most boys, I knew a lot about the different kinds of horses. I knew that the Canadian horse was bred from horses the King of France sent a long time ago from his own stables to the people of Quebec. This mare was true to breed. Not tall, she stood about fifteen hands. With that muscular butt and thick haunches, she could pull the sled all day without tiring.

"I've heard good things about that breed," I said, not letting my excitement show.

"She's ten years old," said Howard, "with a lot of horse sense. You'll like this mare. She's strong, willing, and steady as she goes."

I went up to Labelle, rubbed her nose and let her have a good look at me. She pricked her ears forward and gazed at me with her bright, lively eyes. We didn't need words of introduction. I read in her eyes, and she read in mine, that we were going to be friends.

Labelle seemed as glad as I to start out. The sled moved smoothly. Apart from the occasional shriek of a blue jay flying overhead, the swoosh of the sled's runners and the slapping of the reins were the only sounds as Labelle and I covered the seventeen miles to Fort Erie. It was a sunny day. I was enjoying the drive so much that until I actually reached Fort Erie, I didn't worry about what I'd do next.

But darkness comes early in late December. By the time we reached Fort Erie, my cheerful mood was fading along with the light. Mr. Kemp's list of friends gave clear direction to the home of Mr. Leonard Goodwin, the man who would lodge me and my horse this first night of our journey. At least, I hoped he would!

Mr. Goodwin's house was large, an elegant home just outside the town. It was painted white, with black shutters on the windows. There was a fanlight over the front door, through which a soft glow told me that the lamps had already been lit.

I climbed down from my seat on the sled and stood for a moment by Labelle's head, wondering how this would turn out. "Wish me luck, Labelle," I said, giving her neck a pat before walking up the snow-covered path to the front door. Lifting the brass knocker, which was shaped like a lion's head, I rapped firmly.

Immediately I heard footsteps approach. The door opened, and I was face-to-face with a tall, white-haired gentleman. He had strong features and a well-cut chin beard. "Mr. Goodwin?" I asked.

"I am Leonard Goodwin," His eyes seemed to say, *Who the devil are you?*

I answered his unasked question. "I'm Dory Dickson, and I work for Mr. Sam Kemp. That's his horse and sled outside."

Mr. Goodwin looked past me at Labelle and the sled standing

at the foot of his walk. "Mr. Kemp is my friend. I presume he sent you here. Please explain what this is all about."

"He asks you, as a favour, to give me lodging for the night and stabling for the horse. I'm on my way to Gosfield Township on the north shore of Lake Erie. He's sending me to deliver some goods—a bequest, I guess you'd call it—a spinning wheel and a loom that Mrs. Kemp wanted to leave to her best friend, a lady who lives there."

He looked hard at me. "That's a long journey and a heavy responsibility for a youngster like you."

"Yes,sir. I'm honoured that Mr. Kemp has entrusted me with it." I held out the letter of introduction. "This will explain who I am and what I'm doing."

"Please come in while I read it."

I stepped inside. Mr. Goodwin read the letter quickly. Then he nodded. "Of course I welcome you! Sam Kemp is a special friend, which gives you a special claim to my help." He folded the letter and returned it to me. "We have an hour before dinner. I'll put on my coat and we'll see to your horse. Then you can meet my wife and granddaughter." In a minute he returned, wearing a greatcoat that had two capes over the shoulders, and carrying a lantern. He closed the door behind us, and we walked side by side to the sled.

I took hold of Labelle's bridle and led her, following Mr. Goodwin, around to the back of the house. Together we pulled open the double doors of the carriage house, which was a long, low building. It held a buggy, a wagon and a sleigh. The sleigh was a beauty. Even in the half-light, its black paint gleamed. It was a cabriole sleigh with sleek, low wooden runners and upholstered leather seats. A man had to be wealthy to own a sleigh like that.

In the carriage house there was enough space for my sled. I was glad it would have shelter, even though the tarpaulin cover would have kept the cargo safe from any kind of weather. Mr. Goodwin's carriage house adjoined the stable. When Labelle had been unhitched from the sled, I led her there and put her in a stall. I fetched her water and a measure of oats.

While I rubbed her down, Mr. Goodwin talked to his own horses, a pair of smart-looking bays. He tossed a couple of flakes of hay into the mangers of all three horses.

Now that Labelle was settled, Mr. Goodwin and I returned to the house. After taking off our coats, we went into the parlour, where his wife and granddaughter sat working at their embroidery. They had good light to do their needlework, because the parlour was well lit by several lamps. The lamps had delicate glass shades, some fluted and some shaped like globes with open tops. Ma would have loved one of those lamps. At home we used tallow candles because whale oil was so expensive.

I stood on the Turkish carpet, holding my bundle, while Mr. Goodwin introduced me to his wife and granddaughter. Mrs. Goodwin was a silver-haired old lady dressed in black. To tell the truth, I didn't notice her all that much. It was Miss Laura, the granddaughter, who had my attention. She was about sixteen years old, and the prettiest girl I had ever seen. Her hair was pure gold. But it wasn't just the colour I noticed. At the back, she had her hair twisted into a thick rope and tied up in a knot; in front it was curled into long, drooping ringlets that dangled in front of her ears. She was fair in complexion, with smooth skin and deep blue eyes that looked troubled even though her lips wore a smile.

When Mrs. Goodwin invited me to join them, I sat down on an upholstered chair, my bundle on my lap. She listened with interest as I explained the reason for my journey, and when I had finished, she said, "Mrs. Kemp was a lovely person. I'm glad her husband is so faithfully carrying out her last wishes." Laura kept working at her embroidery and didn't utter a word all the while Mrs. Goodwin and I were talking. From the dreamy look on her face, it appeared that her thoughts were far away.

Mr. Goodwin agreed that Mr. Kemp deserved praise for carrying out his wife's last wishes. He stated again that on such an errand I was welcome in their home. Then he began to fire question after question at me, it soon becoming clear that his interest in Mrs. Kemp's bequest was not nearly as great as his interest in the political situation. He knew about the rout of the Patriots at Montgomery's Tavern in Toronto and about William Lyon Mackenzie raising an army on Navy Island. When I told him about the burning of the *Caroline*, he clapped his hands together with glee. "Good for Allan McNab! Strong action is needed to stop those American rascals from interfering in our politics. As for Mackenzie, he should be hanged for treason."

His outburst was interrupted by the maid, a mouse-like woman in a white apron, announcing that dinner was ready. As soon as we were seated at the table, Mr. Goodwin returned to the same topic with an even more fiery denunciation of the rebels. He praised the lieutenant governor, Sir Francis Bond Head, for refusing to compromise with reformers. Mr. Goodwin's extreme views surprised me. Because Mr. Kemp did not take sides, I took for granted that his friends would do the same. But Mr. Goodwin went on and on to praise the rich families that ran Upper Canada. "If we're to enjoy peace, order and good government," he ranted, "power must remain in the steady hands of a responsible ruling class." He never said the words "Family Compact," but I knew that's who he meant.

He kept speaking this way until suddenly, when he paused for breath, Laura rolled her eyes heavenward and exclaimed. "My Grandfather thinks that politics is the most interesting subject in the whole world!"

Silence greeted these words. Mrs. Goodwin, whose fork was partway to her mouth, lowered it and said quietly. "For gentlemen, it is." Then she turned to me. "Laura would rather live in Toronto than in Fort Erie. She finds us dull."

Laura flushed. "I'm sorry, Grandmother, I shouldn't have said that. But it *is* dull living here. When I think what I'd be doing if I still lived in Toronto! My friends from school write to me about plays and dances and assemblies they attend. Tomorrow there'll be a ball to celebrate New Year's Eve. In Fort Erie, I'm simply starved for pleasures of that kind."

Mr. Goodwin, after being silent since Laura's outburst, said gruffly. "Count yourself fortunate that you're not starved for anything else."

Mrs. Goodwin sounded apologetic as she said to me, "Laura's life here is far different from what she once expected her life to be. Her mother, our daughter, married into one of the best Toronto families, a family prominent in business, politics, the legal profession and the Anglican Church. But disease is no respecter of wealth or position. When Laura was eleven, cholera swept Toronto. Her parents were among the victims. Since then, she has lived with us."

"Grandmother," Laura interrupted. "I am grateful to have a home with you and Grandfather. But I miss the company of girls my age."

"The minister's daughter is exactly your age," said Mrs. Goodwin, "and she has a very sweet nature. She has called on you. I'm sure she's eager to be your friend."

"Oh, Prudence is nice enough," Laura said with a laugh, tossing all her curls. "But she's so . . . mild! I don't believe she reads anything but the Bible."

"Laura," said Mrs. Goodwin, "you shouldn't make fun of Prudence. But I understand how much you miss life in Toronto. I don't blame you. In fact, I believe that a season in Toronto is exactly what you need. You're old enough to be introduced to society. If you're going to make a suitable marriage, it's time for you to meet some suitable young men."

"I can pick a husband for myself," Laura muttered sulkily.

"Of course you can! But there's not much choice around here, unless you want to marry a farmer."

I stared at my plate, feeling my cheeks redden. *My father's a farmer. My grandpa was a farmer. God willing, when I'm a man, I'll be a farmer too.*

I don't remember what we talked about for the rest of dinnertime. Laura didn't even once speak directly to me. When we had left the table, I asked to be excused. I was very tired, I explained, from my day's journey. As we spoke, we were standing in the open double-doorway between the dining room and the parlour. Laura, at her grandmother's shoulder, was facing me. I saw her lift her delicate hand to conceal a yawn. She had white, slender, tapering fingers.

"Will you be leaving us tomorrow?" Mrs. Goodwin asked.

"Yes, ma'am. In the morning. I'd like to reach Anthony's Mills before I stop again."

At the words "Anthony's Mills" Laura gave a jump. She looked at me hard, as if she had something to say. But the moment passed. Mrs. Goodwin summoned the maid to take me to the bedroom where I was to spend the night.

CHAPTER EIGHT

After breakfast, when I was ready to leave, I noticed Laura hanging about, giving me sideways glances that made clear that she wanted to speak to me in private. I was interested, but also alarmed. She looked timid, eager and worried all at the same time. I hadn't the least idea what she wanted with me. So I waited, and she waited.

Mrs. Goodwin brought me a package containing food to eat along the way. After she had said goodbye and Mr. Goodwin had gone to put on his boots and overcoat to go with me to the stable, Laura's chance came.

I was alone in the front hall when she emerged from the parlour, first peering around the doorframe as if there were some kind of danger. Then she came up to me with the sweetest smile on her lips and laid her soft white hand on my arm. I shivered with delight at her touch. She was as pretty as a rose, and she even smelled like a rose.

"Will you do me a favour?" she began.

"Oh, yes, Miss Laura, gladly."

"It's to deliver a letter to my friend who lives in Anthony's Mills. His name is Peter Dash. He works at the sawmill."

According to the list that Mr. Kemp had given me, I'd be staying that night at the home of Mr. Caleb Simpson in Anthony's Mills, which was at the mouth of the Grand River. Since Anthony's Mills was a very small place, I knew that Laura's friend would be easy to find. Yet I was uneasy at her request. I wanted to please Laura, and my parents had brought me up to be helpful. But it was clear that Laura didn't want her grand-parents to know about the letter. Mr. and Mrs. Goodwin had been kind to me. It would be wrong to go behind their backs. On the other hand, I couldn't bear to disappoint this beautiful girl, who was clearly in distress.

"Yes, I'll deliver it for you." I hoped my hesitation hadn't shown.

Then she took her hand from my arm, reached into the top of the bodice of her dress, and pulled out a small ivory-coloured envelope. This action made me blush. When she handed me the envelope and I felt its warmth from her bosom, my face burned even more.

"Put it in your pocket quickly," she whispered. Then she leaned so close that she was speaking in my ear and her soft golden curls brushed my cheek. "Promise you'll deliver it into no other hands but his!"

I gulped, "I promise." I thrust the letter into my pocket, and then I stood back from her while I put on my coat, hat and scarf.

In a few moments Mr. Goodwin joined us. Laura gave me the sweetest smile as I left with him to harness Labelle and hitch up the sled.

This was the second time in two days that I had made a sol-emn promise. The first was to Mr. Kemp when I gave him my word that I would never let anyone see the list of his friends who would help me. I felt fine about that promise. As for this morning's promise to Laura—well, I was glad I hadn't crossed my heart.

* * *

It was a bright clear day, the sky cloudless blue. The white snow sparkled in the sunshine, yet dark gloom covered my heart. Laura's smell of roses had long gone. I passed the morn-ing staring at the landscape, filled with remorse. I wished I had refused to carry the letter. But since I had accepted the trust, I was honour-bound to carry it out. *I'm a sneak*, I thought bitterly.

It entered my mind that I could deliberately lose or destroy the letter. But that would make me a coward as well as a sneak.

By the time I reached Anthony's Mills, I had made up my mind to deliver the letter before looking for the place where I was to spend the night. As soon as I rid myself of the letter, I could put it from my mind. If I saw Laura again on my way back to Chippawa, I could tell her I had kept my promise. That would be the end of the matter.

In the village of Anthony's Mills, the sawmill, the gristmill and the blacksmith shop were all within a stone's throw of one another, but the blacksmith shop was the only one where I saw and heard any sign of action. If Peter Dash worked at the sawmill, that's where I should look for him. But what kind of work could he be doing in the middle of winter, when the great waterwheel stood still and the millpond was frozen over? I saw footprints in the snow leading up to the door, so I knew that somebody must be inside the mill. After tying Labelle to a hitching post in the yard, I opened the door and went in.

Two men were at work. One was working with a file on the teeth of the mill's saw blade.

It was the kind of blade that goes up and down while a couple of fellows push a log through so that the saw cuts the log into planks, one plank at a time. Scritch! Scritch! Scritch! His file rasped against the metal blade. The other man was oiling an iron rod with a greasy rag.

"Hello!" I called to them. "Does one of you happen to be Peter Dash?"

Neither had noticed me until then. They both turned and looked at me. The one working on the sawteeth said, "I'm Peter Dash."

He was about twenty-five years old, tall and slender, and I suppose handsome in the way girls like—wavy dark hair, clean-shaven, black moustache. Even though his work clothes were none too clean, he had a smooth, dandy look about him. His whole appearance was one of confidence, the self-assurance of a man who can do anything he wants and get away with it. I hesitated, unsure how to begin, and then I said simply, "I have a letter for you."

His eyes narrowed. "A letter?"

"From a young lady in Fort Erie."

"Is that right? Let's have it, then." Instead of coming to me, he waited for me to bring the letter to him. Pulling it from my pocket, I caught again Laura's scent of roses. The envelope was clean until Peter Dash's dirty hand took it. He sniffed the envelope, and then he ripped it open.

As he read, a sleek smile spread across his face. The other man put down his oily rag and walked over, edging sideways and craning his neck trying to read the letter over Dash's shoulder. Although the same age as Peter Dash, he was as different from him as a man could be, for he was short, plump and blond.

Dash finished reading the letter, snickered, and handed it to his inquisitive friend. "Take a look at this, Andy!"

I was horrified. Nobody had ever sent me a letter. But if I ever should receive a letter—especially a letter from a girl—I'd never just hand it over for somebody else to read.

Andy's mouth dropped open. His look at Dash was a mixture of amazement and admiration. "Wow! That girl is sure in love with you!"

Dash smirked. "What do you think I should do?"

"She wants to run away with you. Are you going to marry her?"

"I might. She's rich."

Andy laughed, "Well, if you don't want to marry her, I will."

Dash took back the letter. "I didn't say I won't marry her. But I want to have some excitement in my life before I settle down."

"There's no excitement working here," said Andy.

"I know that! But I never planned to spend my life sharpening sawteeth in a lumber mill." Dash thrust the letter into his trousers pocket. "I've been thinking it's time to look for some action. Tomorrow's the start of a new year. William Lyon

Mackenzie is paying recruits one hundred dollars to join his army. I'm going to take him up on that offer. I'll like the adventure, and afterwards I'll sure enjoy having one hundred dollars to spend. When it's gone, I think I will marry the girl. As soon as Laura's married to me, everything she owns is mine. That's the law."

Now he looked at me. "You can tell Laura that I'll—"

"Woah! Just a minute!" I was burning with indignation. "I'm not taking any message back to Miss Laura. I brought you her letter as a favour to her because I was passing through Anthony's Mills anyway. But even if I were going right back to Fort Erie, I sure wouldn't be your messenger boy." Without waiting for him to answer, I turned on my heels and marched right out of there.

Labelle looked pleased to see me. It was now late afternoon. She seemed to know that her day's work was nearly done and a scoop of oats awaited her at the next stop. My anger soon cooled. I felt a sensation of freedom to have carried out my promise to Laura, although I felt anxious for her. Somebody should warn her about Peter Dash.

CHAPTER NINE

ow I had to find the home of Caleb Simpson. That should not be difficult. A fast-moving sleigh raced by its bells jingle-jangling. The sleigh was driven by a young man, a girl seated beside him.

I called out to them, "Can you tell me where Caleb Simpson lives?"

They didn't hear me, but the sleigh stopped only a hundred yards further on, in front of the finest log cabin I had ever seen. It was two storeys high, with a covered verandah all the way across the front. It looked like the sort of place where one of Mr. Kemp's friends might live. So I brought my sled up beside the sleigh and shouted, "Is this the home of Caleb Simpson?"

The young man shouted back, as he helped the girl from the sleigh, "No. Squire William Anthony lives here. Simpson's place is over there," and he pointed to the last house in the village, standing alone. Behind it was an outbuilding, a field, and then the forest.

I thanked the young man for directing me. Simpson's log cabin wasn't nearly as attractive as Mr. Goodwin's fine home, where I had stayed the night before. This was a disappointment, since I suppose I had taken for granted that all of Mr. Kemp's friends lived in comfort.

I stopped Labelle in front of this last house. Smoke rose from the chimney. Despite this evidence that somebody lived there, I had an odd feelings that the place was uninhabited. I climbed down from my seat on the sled, walked up to the door, and knocked. Hearing no sound within, I knocked again. This time there was a response. Shuffling footsteps approached. I heard the drawing of a bolt and the door was stealthily opened, but only partway. The man who stood in the doorway was old and bent. His rumpled grey shirt lacked several buttons. Shaggy white side-whiskers framed his face. He peered at me suspiciously with little beady black eyes. "What do you want?"

"Are you Mr. Simpson?"

"Yes."

"If you please . . . Holding out the letter of introduction that Mr. Kemp had given me, I began in a rush of words, "Mr. Sam Kemp has sent me from Chippawa on personal business of his. I'm on my way to Gosfield Township to deliver some things that belonged to his late wife. He'd appreciate it if you'd give me lodging for the night."

Simpson took the letter but did not invite me to enter. He read it, handed it back and closed the door in front of my face. I heard the bolt click into place.

Shocked and discouraged, I returned to the sled. I sat on the board seat, wondering what to do. Maybe there was an inn in Anthony's Mills where I could stay. Mr. Kemp had supplied me with money. I would need it tonight.

Then I saw a ragged curtain twitch at the window, and a few moments later I heard the bolt drawn again. This time the door opened wider. "Kemp takes a lot for granted," the old man growled. "But I can't leave your horse to freeze in the cold."

I was about ready to fall on my knees with gratitude. "Thank you, sir!"

"Don't thank me," he grunted. "Wait till I put on my coat."

When he joined me, he led the way to the outbuilding behind the cabin. It was a drive shed and stable combined. There was no room for the sled, but there were two stalls. A tall grey gelding was in one, and the other was empty.

I unhitched Labelle, led her into the stable and put her in the empty stall. Mr. Simpson tossed a few flakes of hay into the manger and filled the water bucket. The grey gelding watched with his ears laid back, looking just as unwelcoming as his owner.

"I'll see you indoors when you've got her settled," Mr. Simpson left without another word. After rubbing down Labelle and brushing her thick mane and tail, I checked her feet. Everything looked fine.

Darkness had fallen by the time I joined Mr. Simpson in the cabin. The main room was lit by one smoky tallow candle and warmed by an iron stove, on which he heated up a stew of chicken, carrots and potatoes. Famished, I tucked right into it and emptied my bowl before Mr. Simpson was half finished his. As he ate, he looked up at me from time to time with his black beady eyes. Although the candle gave little light, he certainly could see through the gloom that my bowl was empty. I waited for him to offer me a second helping, but he never did. There was no conversation. He didn't ask how Mr. Kemp was faring, or what was happening in Chippawa, or anything about the rebellion.

When he had finished eating, he stood up from the table, walked across the floor to a settee that stood over against the wall, lifted the lid and took out two blankets. He lowered the lid of the settee, "This is where you sleep. You'll be leaving first thing in the morning."

This was a statement, not a question. He took the candle with him into the cabin's other room, leaving me in the dark. I folded the one blanket to use as a pillow, lay down on the settee and covered myself with the other blanket. When the fire in the stove died down, the room became bitterly cold. I was awake shivering for much of the night.

In the morning Mr. Simpson built up the fire in the stove and boiled water for tea. We had fried bread for breakfast. He gave me a slice of fried bread to take with me.

I was glad to leave, even though a cold wind gusted from the west, lifting loose snow from the ice surface and blowing it in my face as Labelle and I crossed the frozen Grand River.

CHAPTER TEN

My next stop along the Talbot Road would be at a place called Williamsville, where my host would be Mr. Thomas Hoover. I prayed that my stay in Williamsville would be more pleasant than my time in Anthony's Mills had been. Although I could put Mr. Simpson's cold reception and cold cabin behind me, I couldn't forget my meeting with Peter Dash. What a scoundrel! Poor Laura! How could she fall in love with someone like that? I hoped that Peter Dash would go off to join Mackenzie's army on Navy Island and never come back. Whatever happened, somebody had to stop Laura from marrying him.

As the day went on, the wind subsided and the sky cleared. The road to Williamsville passed through several villages—Cayuga, Sweet's Corners, Rainham Centre. Between these villages were prosperous-looking farms. Pa had told me that Colonel Talbot settled thirty thousand people along this road. If I stopped working for Mr. Kemp, it likely would be easy for me to find employment in one of these settlements. But Chippawa was close to home. When this journey was finished and I returned to the work Mr. Kemp had hired me for—chopping wood and tending fires—I'd be able to visit my family from time to time. That's what I wanted to do.

I reached Williamsville in the late afternoon. It looked like a fine village. I stopped in front of the general store, tied Labelle to the hitching post and went inside. Three men were standing around the iron stove, talking. The storekeeper, wearing a canvas apron, was behind the wide wooden counter. Stacked on shelves behind him were all manner of goods, from rubber boots to jugs of molasses. Everyone looked up when I entered.

"Excuse me," I said. "I'm looking for the home of Mr. Thomas Hoover. Can you direct me to it?"

The men standing by the stove exchanged glances. For a moment nobody uttered a word.

Finally, the storekeeper said, "It's the big, white frame house right across the street from the church. You can't miss it."

That sounded good. I hoped that Mr. Hoover would be as hospitable as Mr. Goodwin had been. Yet I wondered about that moment of hesitation before my question received an answer. I returned to the sled and set out. Mr. Hoover's home was easy to find, as the storekeeper had said it would be, right across the main street from the church. To the left of the house's wide verandah there was a driveway leading to a small stable at the rear. The driveway was covered by an unbroken blanket of snow. I stopped Labelle at the verandah, promised her I'd be back in a couple of minutes, and went up to the front door.

I rapped firmly with the shiny brass knocker, and then listened as quick, light footsteps approached. The door was opened by a girl no older than me, wearing a white frilled cap and a white apron. She had pink cheeks, and grey eyes with a touch of green.

"Good afternoon, Miss," I said. "I've come to see Mr. Hoover."

She took a quick breath. "I'm so sorry . . . but . . . Mr. Hoover is . . . was . . ." She cleared her throat and said softly "Mr. Hoover died." She lowered her eyes.

"Oh."

She raised her eyes and her voice. "Would you like to speak to Mrs. Hoover?"

What should I do? Mr. Hoover must have died recently, if Mr. Kemp didn't know about his death. At last I managed to say that I *would* like to speak to Mrs. Hoover, though my mind was in turmoil about what I would say. I also felt dismay, because the prospect of spending the night in this fine house began to vanish before my eyes. The girl opened the door wider. I stepped inside and stamped the snow from my boots.

The girl did not leave to fetch Mrs. Hoover as I expected she would. Instead, she stood watching me until, after a long moment, she said, "Would you like to take off your coat and boots?" From this suggestion I realized that she meant to take me to Mrs. Hoover, not bring Mrs. Hoover to me. So I doffed my coonskin hat, unwound my long scarf from my neck, pulled off my coat and my boots, and followed her.

She led me to the dining room, where an old lady sat at the table, looking as though she were about to start eating. By the light of two tall candles in silver candlesticks, I saw that the table was laid for one person, with a teapot, a cup of tea already poured, a small platter of sandwiches, and several cupcakes on a china plate. The old lady's dress was black, and she wore a black lace widow's cap over her white hair. She regarded me through steel-rimmed spectacles of such thickness that her eyes appeared huge.

I looked humbly at the tasteful table setting and held out my letter from Mr. Kemp as if it were an offering. "This is a letter from Mr. Sam Kemp in Chippawa, introducing me. My name is Theodore Dickson. Everybody calls me Dory"

"What brings you here?" She took the letter from my hand.

"I'm on my way to Albertville in Gosfield Township to take a loom and spinning wheel to the best friend of Mr. Kemp's late wife. It was Mrs. Kemp's dying wish that her friend should have them. Mr. Kemp was sure that your husband would put up me and my horse for one night along the way."

Mrs. Hoover read the letter and handed it back to me. Raising her head, she regarded me with her magnified eyes. "My husband died just before Christmas. He would gladly have given you lodging for the night. If for no other reason, he would have done so as a favour to me, because Mr. Kemp's wife Margaret was my dear niece. So of course, I am happy to have you stay here. You have arrived uninvited, but you are very welcome."

A flood of relief passed through me from head to toe. "Thank you, Ma'am."

"Not at all. I'm glad to be of help in carrying out my niece's last wishes. What puzzles me is the substance of Margaret's bequest. I didn't know that she owned a loom and spinning wheel. But then, it's been years since I last paid her a visit. She must have acquired them since then. Yet she never mentioned them in one of her letters." Mrs. Hoover laughed. "It's odd. But it doesn't matter. Please take your horse to the stable. Pagan and Slow Poke will be glad of the company. I'm sure they're lonely, even though I have a local boy come twice a day to look after them. In horse years, they're as old as I am. Like me, they hardly ever get out and about. After you've taken care of your horse, you may join me for supper." Now she spoke to the girl. "Vera, see that Dory has everything he needs."

"Yes, Mrs. Hoover."

Vera acted prim and proper, standing with her head lowered as long as we were in the dining room; but as soon as we had left, she raised her chin and gave me a wink. It was an unmistakable wink, not just the effect of something caught in her eye. I'd never had a girl wink at me before. She smiled as she held up my coat to help me put it on. "See you soon!" She said cheerfully when I went outside to take Labelle to the stable.

Labelle received just as warm a welcome in the stable as I had received in the house. Pagan and Slow Poke, two fat old horses with dusty manes, leaned out of their stalls, craning their necks to take a good look at her. They watched while I rubbed her down and checked her feet. When I fed Labelle, I gave each of them a few flakes of hay as well, and then I left Labelle to become acquainted with her neighbours.

When I returned to the dining room, Mrs. Hoover was still at the table. Vera had now set a second place. When I was seated, she brought in a fresh pot of tea and a fresh supply of sandwiches and cupcakes. The hot tea, the food and the warmth of the room all combined to make me feel lightheaded. As I sipped and ate, Mrs. Hoover plied me with questions about myself, her huge eyes watching my face as I answered. *She sees everything,* I thought. *She understands.* And so I found myself telling her about our poor farm, and my brothers who died, and little Susan, and how I wanted to buy a new horse to pull the plough so we wouldn't lose the farm. By the time we had finished supper, Mrs. Hoover knew all my hopes and dreams.

While we were eating, Vera made up a bedroom for me, with a fire in the fireplace. After supper Mrs. Hoover, leaning on her cane, took me there. When she had left, I took a look around. A small oil lamp on the fireplace shelf gave plenty of light. The four-poster bed was covered with a colourful quilt. There was hot water in the pitcher on the washstand, and a china chamber pot behind a screen. I went to the window, pulled the curtain aside and looked out. I saw the stable, where Labelle was resting. Two or three stars twinkled in the sky, and I thanked my lucky stars for bringing me here.

After I had put out the lamp and gone to bed, I thought about Vera and the way she had winked at me. She was not as beautiful as Laura. She smelled not of roses but of onions. But Vera was pretty enough, with her grey-green eyes and pink cheeks. I went to sleep feeling pleased with myself and with my good fortune.

I did not see Mrs. Hoover in the morning. "She always sleeps late," Vera explained as she set before me a bountiful breakfast of bacon and eggs, fried potatoes, buttered bread and strawberry jam. While I was eating, she made sandwiches for me to take with me, wrapping them in paper and tying the package with a red ribbon. She gave it to me with a smile and then followed me to the door and helped me to put on my coat.

My long, knitted scarf fascinated her. "I've never seen such a long scarf," she said as she began to wrap it around my neck. "It must be at least six feet long."

"It is," I said. "My mother knitted it. When it was as long as it needed to be, she still had half a ball of red wool to use up. So she just kept on knitting till it was gone."

I felt my cheeks turn as red as my scarf while she wound it around and around my neck, circling me, and every circle brought her closer. By the time she had finished, her nose was two inches from mine. I thanked her for her help.

"You may kiss me, if you like," Vera said.

When she said these words, I became so confused that I didn't know what to do or say.

So I gave her a peck on the cheek and fled.

All that day I thought about Vera, off and on, as Labelle and I made our way west along the Talbot Road. I wondered whether I had done the right thing by kissing her on the cheek.

Never before had any girl ever shown interest in me. It made me feel excited in a way that was completely new.

CHAPTER ELEVEN

Day followed day, and every day brought me closer to my destination. Although some of Mr. Kemp's friends were less welcoming than others, none turned me away. I stayed one night at a farm where Labelle was lodged in a barn with only pigs for company, and another night when the lack of a bed forced me to sleep with her in a stable. I spent one night in the village of Tillsonburg, and the next in St. Thomas.

There were times when I questioned the purpose of this long journey. But if the bequest to her friend had meant that much to Mrs. Kemp and if Mr. Kemp was willing to trust his horse and sled to a fourteen-year-old boy, then it wasn't my business to criticize. On the whole, I was enjoying myself, seeing places I had never seen before. For my first week, nothing went wrong. But on the eighth day, it did.

It was late afternoon, and we had about three miles to go to our next stop, which would be at the tavern in a village called Morpeth, when Labelle began to limp. The problem seemed to be with her right front hoof. I stopped the sled and got down from my seat to talk to her. "Does it hurt, Labelle? Do you need to rest your foot?" She didn't need words to tell me. The look in her eyes and way she snorted and breathed and pushed her head against my shoulder told me that she could not go on.

In my pocket I had ten dollars that Mr. Kemp had given me for unexpected expenses. It looked as though I was going to need that money. What I had to do was knock at the door of the nearest farmhouse and ask the farmer to put us up for a day or two until my horse's hoof was better. I didn't know what was wrong with her foot but hoped it was only a bruise.

I had stopped the sled right in front of a place that might do. It was a small log house standing back from the road, with a pump in the front yard. Behind the house were a barn and an outhouse. I didn't get back on the sled but walked beside Labelle, leading her by her bridle, up to the house. With a pat on the neck, I left her, approached the door and knocked.

A moment later, a man opened the door. He had pale skin, messy black hair and a wild beard. He wore a long, loose shirt that was smeared with paint in many colours—red, yellow, grey, blue—a whole rainbow. Closely behind him, and peering over his shoulder, was a young woman. With her freckled cheeks and her ginger hair tied back with a string, she looked about twenty years old.

They glanced at me, and then beyond me at the horse and sled. "What can we do for you?" the man said.

"My horse has gone lame. I aimed to be in Morpeth by the end of the day, but she can't go any further until I've seen to her foot."

The man opened the door wider. "Step inside. It's cold out there."

The door opened directly upon the kitchen. There was a cast-iron stove, a table, a settee, a few chairs and a rag rug on the floor. Although the furniture was the kind you would see in any farm kitchen, there was one surprising item—a stand on which rested an unfinished painting of something that looked like a tower.

The girl saw me looking at the picture. "Ralph's an artist," she said.

"That's me," said the man. "Ralph Butler. Miranda's my wife."

I introduced myself, saying that Labelle was my horse, which wasn't strictly true, but good enough for now.

"We can't leave her out there," said Ralph. "We'll put her in the barn. There's a stall."

Ralph donned his coat and hat, and we went outside to unhitch Labelle and put her in the barn. There were two stalls. One held a cow, and the other was empty. There were no other animals, apart from a few chickens, who cackled irritably from their nesting boxes, annoyed at having their peace disturbed.

Labelle settled gratefully into her stall and accepted a meal of water and hay. I told Ralph I should see to her foot right away. "That's a good idea," he said, "come back to the house when you're done."

After he had gone, I took a careful look at Labelle's right front hoof. What had happened wasn't clear to me; there are many things that can cause a bruise. A good night's rest might clear up the problem, so long as an abscess hadn't formed. I told Labelle that I'd see her in the morning.

When I returned to the house, Miranda was cooking supper. "Will you join us?" she said.

"With pleasure."

Soon the three of us were gathered around the table over a meal of potatoes, turnips and fried chicken. While we ate, I told them the reason for my journey. Miranda said that she wished she had a loom, but a spinning wheel wouldn't be much use without sheep to shear for wool.

After supper I raised the subject of payment, and we agreed that one dollar a night was fair. I supposed that I'd be staying with Ralph and Miranda for only a day or two. Even if my stay proved a little longer, the ten dollars that Mr. Kemp had given me would be enough.

The food was delicious, and I told them how much I was enjoying it. "Miranda's the provider," Ralph said. "She looks after the chickens, milks the cow, churns butter, grows potatoes and turnips. I'd starve if it weren't for Miranda."

I saw her looking at him with the most loving and worshipful gaze. "Ralph's an artist," she said, for the second time. A look of shared adoration passed between them.

"I like pictures," I said, "especially pictures of nature." As I said it, I realized that this was the truth, even though I had never actually thought about it before.

"In the morning," said Ralph, "you can see by daylight what I've done. I have a stack of canvases that I haven't sold."

"More's the pity," Miranda sighed. She rose from the table and lit a candle, for the room had become quite dark while we were eating. By candlelight Miranda looked very pretty, although pale and slightly weary. Wisps had escaped from the string that held back her ginger hair, and now they trailed in little curls down her slender neck.

After supper, Ralph washed the dishes and Miranda dried them. I'd never before seen a man wash dishes. He didn't look embarrassed to be doing woman's work. I supposed that artists must be different from ordinary folks.

The house had two bedrooms, which was another surprise. Both bedrooms opened off the kitchen. Miranda showed me the room that would be mine. "This will be the children's room," she said with a smile, "when we have some."

It was a pleasant little room, with curtains on the window, a bed, a chair and a washstand.

A large china pitcher rested beside a basin on the washstand. Miranda filled the pitcher with water so that I might wash myself in the morning. Worrying about Labelle kept me awake for a long time.

CHAPTER TWELVE

When I awoke, my first thoughts were of Labelle. I threw back the coverlet, jumped out of bed, washed and pulled on my clothes. There was no sound of anyone stirring. I opened my bedroom door, tiptoed cross the kitchen and quietly left the house. In the frail early morning light, a few snowflakes drifted like feathers through the still air.

Labelle whinnied to see me. I gave her hay and water. When she had eaten, I took her from her stall to let her walk around. Her limp was worse. I bent over and picked up her hoof. The whole foot area felt hot. "I'm going to get a bucket of warm water to soak your foot," I told her, and I put her into her stall. I started back to the house, meeting Miranda on her way to the barn, an empty metal pail swinging from her hand.

"Good morning. It's milking time," she said cheerfully. I followed her back into the barn, explaining why I needed a bucket of warm water. "As soon as I've finished the milking," she said, "we can heat some on the stove." While she milked the cow, I mucked out Labelle's stall and tossed in a few forkfuls of fresh straw. I carried the pail of milk back to the house for Miranda. She found another pail and sent me to the pump to fill it with water. But there wasn't room for my pail on top of the stove until after she had made porridge for our breakfast.

When breakfast was over and the water heated, I carried the pail out to the barn. Labelle seemed grateful when I lowered her foot into the warm water. I think it eased her pain. I stayed with her, both to keep her company and to prevent her from accidentally tipping over the pail. After fifteen minutes or so, I lifted her foot from the water. Then I brushed her thick, dark mane and tail.

Miranda came back to the barn to gather eggs. After she left, I was alone with Labelle, the cow and the chickens. I stretched out on a heap of straw and almost fell asleep. All morning I stayed with Labelle and then left the barn to dump the cold water and refill the pail at the pump. I carried the filled pail into the kitchen.

Miranda was making butter, pumping the dasher up and down in the wooden churn.

Ralph was working on the painting that I had noticed the day before. With sunlight streaming through the kitchen window, I now saw clearly that the tower in Ralph's picture was a lighthouse standing on a sandy beach. The top looked snow-white against the blue sky. Near the base of the lighthouse lay a dead tree that had drifted onto the beach. Stripped of its bark, the wood was as white as bone. There were little waves lapping at the shore. Sunshine sparkled on the water. I don't know how Ralph did it, but the picture left no doubt this was a summer day. I could feel the warmth.

Ralph was putting some clouds in the sky. "Where is that?" I asked. "Is it a real lighthouse, or one you imagine?"

His brush stopped moving. "It's real all right. That's the lighthouse on Pelee Island, built four years ago. I made the sketch last summer when I was back home visiting my parents. Now I'm doing it with oil paints."

I watched while he fluffed up a cloud and added a bird— a tiny black V-shaped mark, but it looked just like a gull in flight. "I come from Pelee Island.," he told me as he painted. "My parents are tenants of William McCormick. He owns the whole island. It's a very peaceful place, although that's likely to change. There's a rumour that William Lyon Mackenzie's Patriots plan to take over Pelee Island as a first step to invading Canada."

"Let's not speak of that," said Miranda, "I'm tired of hearing about Patriots."

Ralph laid down his brush. "Let me show you another painting of Pelee Island. This is one I've finished." He went to an open wooden box that stood against the wall and pulled out a big picture of water and a rock. The rock was in the water, but close to shore. The water looked choppy, grey and cold.

"There's a story to go with this one," Ralph said. "It's called *Hulda's Rock*. Hulda was an Indian girl who lived long ago on Pelee Island, daughter of a chief. She was betrayed by an Englishman. He married her according to the custom of her people. After a while he returned to England, promising to return. She waited and waited. When it was clear that she had been abandoned, she leapt from that rock to drown herself." He put the picture back in the box. "When I painted it, I hoped Mr. McCormick would buy it to hang in his home, but he wasn't interested."

I didn't like to say so, but if I had money to buy a picture for Ma to hang on the wall, I wouldn't choose that one. It was too gloomy. Ralph returned to his painting. Miranda went on pumping the dasher. When the water in my pail was warm, I carried it to the barn and soaked Labelle's foot again.

I had dinner with Ralph and Miranda. Just before bedtime I returned to the barn to check Labelle's hoof. No improvement. But I knew it might take several days of rest and soaking for time to take care of the matter.

In the morning, when I left the house to check on Labelle, I found Miranda standing in the lane beside the sled, looking at the load it carried. There was a skiff of snow on the tarpaulin.

"I can't see the shape of a spinning wheel or a loom under that cover," she said thoughtfully, "It could be a load of firewood, for all I can tell."

"Most likely the loom and spinning wheel were taken apart to make them easier to carry," I said. "I wasn't present to see the sled being loaded, so I don't know."

"May I take a peek?"

"I'm sorry, but Mr. Kemp warned me not to loosen the ropes. The way the tarpaulin is lashed down, the load is safe from any kind of weather."

"You're right," Miranda said. "You need to keep it tight and dry. I was just curious what the loom looked like. I'm saving my money to buy a loom."

She was on her way to milk the cow. I went with her. Labelle was glad to see me. She pricked her ears forward and ate some hay, but her eyes were not as bright and clear as they should be. When I checked her foot, it felt even hotter than the day before, and she winced when I prodded with my finger. I took her from her stall to walk about. Her limp was bad. Labelle was in trouble. We were both in trouble. I had sixty miles still to go to reach Jacob's Fox's farm, and my horse was lame.

CHAPTER THIRTEEN

My father complained about the expense of a farrier," I told Miranda, "but he always managed to find the money when our horse needed care. 'A lame horse,' Pa used to say, 'is good for nothing.'"

Miranda, sitting on the milking stool and pulling at the cow's teats, mumbled, "uh-huh." For a minute or so, the only sound was the splashing of milk into the metal pail. *Psht. Psht Psht.* I broke the silence.

"To me, Labelle isn't just horsepower to pull the sled. She's a friend."

"Even if she is your friend, she still has to pull the sled." *Psht. Psht Psht.*

I didn't answer. This was the third day I'd been staying with Miranda and Ralph. That was three dollars for lodging, according to our agreement. Maybe I should spend a few dollars on a farrier instead of using up Mr. Kemp's money just waiting for nature to heal Labelle's foot.

The sound of splashing milk ceased. Miranda rose from her stool and lifted the pail from under the cow. "I'm going to Morpeth this morning to post a letter. The farrier's place is on my way. I can stop by and ask him to come."

This offer made up my mind for me. "Will you, please?"

"Breakfast comes first," said Miranda. I carried her milk pail to the house for her.

After breakfast, Miranda put on her boots and pulled her grey, threadbare cloak about her narrow shoulders. "The sun

is shining," she said. "It will be a lovely morning for a walk."
She fastened the clasp of her cloak. "It's just three miles to Morpeth. I'll speak to the farrier and be back by noon."

When she had left, I put the pail of water for Labelle's foot on top of the stove. While it heated, I watched Ralph paint. He was adding finishing touches to the top part of the lighthouse, which he called the lantern. Its walls were glass panes. After stepping back to give the lantern a critical look, he dabbed one of the panes with white; instantly the glass gleamed with a flash of sunshine.

Again he stepped back, his brush uplifted and a satisfied expression on his face. "It cost a fortune to build this lighthouse—more than seven hundred pounds, even though Squire McCormick donated the land it's built on and the limestone for the tower. When I was a boy growing up on Pelee Island, I can't tell you the number of ships that were wrecked navigating the Pelee Passage. The *Sylph*, the *Liberty*, the *Macedonian*, then the *Guerriere*."

"What made it so dangerous?" I asked.

"Shoals and reefs. Treacherous currents. There's a string of islands all the way from Pelee Island to Sandusky, Ohio. Middle Island. North Bass Island. Middle Bass Island. Put-in Bay, Kelley's Island. The proper word for it is archipelago. I call it the graveyard of Lake Erie. Oh, that lighthouse was sorely needed! Already it's saved many lives."

"What provides the light? I asked.

"Twelve lamps up there in the lantern. Each has a lens in front and a mirror behind. On a clear night, you can see the light for nine miles in every direction." He paused. "That is, you can see it as long as there's whale oil to keep the lamps burning. Squire McCormick is responsible for the lighthouse. He complains that there isn't a reliable supply."

Now Ralph leaned forward, his eyes narrowed, concentrating on every brush stroke. I don't think he noticed when I left, carrying my pail of warm water out to the barn.

It was my lucky day, because the farrier was free to come right away. He arrived by sleigh late in the morning, bringing Miranda as his passenger. The jangle of his sleigh bells brought me out from the barn. Miranda was all smiles, having posted her letter and enjoyed the sleigh ride home.

Introductions were brief. Miranda had already told the farrier where I had come from and where I was going. His name was Joe Smith. He was a tough, stringy-looking man, a trifle stooped. Apart from a little grey at the temples, his hair was black. His clean-shaven face was just as leathery as the heavy apron that he wore. This apron was in two parts, one covering each leg.

"Let's see the horse," he said, his manner businesslike. Miranda went into the house. Smith and I entered the barn. As soon as he took one look at Labelle, he nodded his approval. "She's a Canadian horse. I like this breed. They're tough and they're eager."

Smith undid his pack of tools: pliers, tweezers, clippers, rasps and a hammer. While I held Labelle's halter, he positioned himself, stooping under her head while facing her tail, and lifted her right front foot, holding it slightly bent. His hands were square, his fingers blunt.

"She's had good care," he said. "Hoof well-trimmed. Shoe fits nicely. But it has to come off." He pulled off her shoe with his pliers. Then he picked up a different tool. It looked like a giant pair of tweezers. "This is the tester." With it he squeezed and poked the underside of Labelle's sore foot. She endured this patiently, until he must have touched the sore spot, because suddenly she jerked her foot and flinched.

"Here it is," he said. "She bruised the sole of her foot. It's hard to tell what caused it. Likely a chunk of ice." Now he raised her uninjured, left front foot. "She's shod on just her front feet. If I take off one shoe, I have to take off both. When her bruised foot clears up, I'll put the same shoes back on again." With his pliers he pulled off the shoe from Labelle's sound hoof.

Then he emerged from under her, straightened his shoulders and stretched. "How have you been treating her foot?"

"Twice a day I soak it for about fifteen minutes in a pail of warm water. Every day I walk her around inside the barn. Most of the time, she rests."

"That's the best way to treat it. From the heat, I know there's an abscess. When it breaks, you'll see pus coming out from the coronet band. That's the hairline just above the hoof. As the abscess drains, the pain will lessen. But you still have to keep soaking the foot. I'll be back in one week to see how she's doing. If all is well, I'll put the shoes back on." He packed up his tools. "My fee for today's visit is two dollars."

I paid him and thanked him for coming so promptly to treat Labelle. But as Smith drove away, my heart sank. The ten dollars that Mr. Kemp had given me was not enough. One more week's lodging here would cost me seven dollars. Then the fee for the farrier's next visit would probably be two more dollars. What was I going to do?

CHAPTER FOURTEEN

After the jingle of the farrier's sleigh bells faded away, I picked up the two shoes he had taken from Labelle's front feet and put them in a safe place. Then I spent a few minutes talking with Labelle. We didn't speak in words, but I read her eyes, and she read mine. Labelle didn't like the delay, she told me. She wanted to be back on the road. She trusted me to do whatever was needed for this to happen.

She trusted me. What must I do to deserve that trust? Well, first of all, I needed to soak her foot. So after giving her neck a pat, I picked up the pail of cold water from her last soaking, carried it outside to dump it, refilled it from the pump and carried it into the house.

Ralph was working at his painting. Miranda was peeling potatoes. They both looked up when I entered. "What did the farrier say?" Miranda asked.

"We'll be here for another week at least," I said gloomily. Then, not wanting to put it off, I grasped the nettle. "I'm so sorry, but I don't have enough money to pay for that many nights."

There! I had said what needed to be said. Miranda and Ralph had taken in a stranger, and now it looked as though they were stuck with me on their hands. I knew they were short of money.

A look passed between them. Like Labelle and me, neither needed words to know what the other was thinking. Miranda spoke first. "Dory, you'd be welcome as our guest even without payment. But since it's been agreed that you will pay, could you not work for your lodging?" She looked in Ralph's direction.

"My husband's art leaves him no time for splitting logs and chopping kindling. Your horse needs a lot of care, but if you could spend an hour here and an hour there, in one week you could build us a woodpile that will last until spring. A cord of firewood costs two dollars if we have to buy it. That adds up to a lot of money you could save us."

Ralph looked pleased at this suggestion. He pointed with his brush at the nearly empty wood box beside the stove. "It's hard for me to keep it filled. So if you could . . ."

If I could! My spirits soared. *Show me the axe and splitting wedge!*

"Yes!" was all I had to say.

"As if Ralph and I would send you away!" Miranda laughed as she put a peeled potato into the pot. "You and your lovely horse!"

I found myself laughing too, partly with relief and partly because I should have known that this was the kind of solution she and Ralph would offer. But that night, before I fell asleep, my thoughts turned to Mr. Kemp and my journey, and again I began to worry. I had set out from Chippawa on the thirtieth of December. I counted on my fingers. Today was the ninth of January. By now I should have reached Jacob Fox's farm in Gosfield Township, unloaded the loom and spinning wheel, and started on my way back to Chippawa. But here I was, with sixty miles to go and a horse that wouldn't be ready to pull the sled for at least a week. I knew that Mr. Kemp trusted me. But still . . . how many weeks would pass before he would see me and his horse and sled again?

As it happened, Miranda found other chores for me to do as well as build up the wood pile. All that week she kept me busy. I churned butter. I scoured the milk pail. For one entire day I helped her to make candles. These were not stubby tallow candles like my mother made in her candle mould. Miranda's beeswax candles were slender and tapered. She showed me how to dip a wick into a pail of melted beeswax and then plunge it into a pail of icy water, before immersing it in hot beeswax again. I had to repeat this process twenty times to make each candle. My first attempts were lumpy and pear-shaped, but I soon got the knack and worked at it until my candles were almost as beautifully tapered as the ones Miranda made. Miranda sold her candles, she told me, to the owner of the Morpeth general store. He was eager to purchase all that she made.

"You're an artist, too," I said to her. .

She blushed. "Oh, no! It's just something I've learned to do. Ralph's the artist."

But nobody buys his paintings, I thought. *You're the one who puts food on the table.*

Miranda's dream, she confided, was for Ralph to have a studio, a small, separate cabin with a big window where he would set up his easel. "Then he can paint in solitude, undisturbed by the children . . . when we have some." She said this with a slightly weary smile.

Ralph's paintings certainly were beautiful. He had about twenty in what he called his portfolio. I'm not sure whether he had ever sold any, and I didn't like to ask. If I had had any money, I would gladly have bought one for my mother. Ma would love to have a picture to hang on the wall.

After five days of twice-daily soaking, the abscess broke. The pus and blood oozing from the hairline above Labelle's right front hoof was a welcome sight to see. Labelle's eyes looked brighter, and she did not limp when I took her from her stall to walk around the barn.

When the farrier, Joe Smith, returned at the end of the week, he pronounced Labelle almost fit to go. "Give it two more days," he said, "then don't push her."

"Can she go as far as Morpeth the first day?"

"Yes. But no further. Those three miles will be enough. After that, use your judgement. Better still, use *her* judgement. She'll let you know when it's time to quit for the day."

Smith hammered the shoes back onto Labelle's front feet, charged me two dollars for the visit, and gave Labelle a carrot as a treat before he left.

CHAPTER FIFTEEN

Two days later, I harnessed Labelle, hitched up the sled and went into the house to say goodbye.

Ralph was standing at his easel. He had started a new painting. Pencil lines suggested two people walking along a shore. "That's Fishing Point," Ralph said. "It's the south tip of Pelee Island—at the opposite end from the lighthouse. You can see North Bass Island in the distance."

I squinted, but all I could see in the distance was a dot on the horizon line. I was peering at this dot when Miranda walked into the kitchen. She was wearing her cloak, and she had a basket over her arm.

"Please," she said to me, "may I ride with you to Morpeth? I have candles ready to deliver. After you've let me off at the general store, I can walk home."

I was happy both to have her company and also to repay some of her kindness. I thanked Ralph for his hospitality, bade him farewell, and left him to his painting.

"Two dozen beeswax candles," Miranda said cheerfully as she climbed onto the sled. She set the basket between us on the board seat. "That's two dollars. I'm going to ask the storekeeper to order white and blue powders for Ralph to mix his paints. He always needs white and blue for painting water and sky."

Labelle, eager to start out, gave an impatient shake to her harness. I put her into a brisk trot. The sled glided smoothly over the packed snow, and we reached Morpeth in less than an hour. We stopped in front of the general store. Miranda gave me a friendly kiss on the cheek before clambering down from the sled with her basket. Before entering the store, she turned and waved good-bye. "Safe journey!" she called to me.

It was not yet noon, too early to stop for the night. But three miles was as far as Labelle should pull the sled today. According to the list Mr. Kemp had given me, my host in Morpeth would be Mr. George Little, the owner of the Morpeth tavern. I liked the idea of staying at a tavern. In the public room there would be people for me to talk to. I was eager to learn the latest news about the rebellion. Ralph and Miranda lived in their own world, apart from politics. During the entire eleven days I had stayed with them, the only mention of Patriots had been Miranda's mild warning not to talk about them.

Morpeth was a pleasant little town. As well as a general store, it had a church, a school, a blacksmith shop and Mr. Little's tavern. The tavern was the largest building on the main street, with both an upper gallery and a ground-level verandah. In front of the tavern were a drinking trough, the water frozen solid, and a hitching rack for horses. The tavern's stable was behind the main building. I drove the sled around to the stable yard. "I'll be back in a few minutes," I said to Labelle, and I left her and the sled standing there while I went into the tavern to look for Mr. Little.

The tavern's public room was furnished with a huge sideboard and many small tables. There was a stack of newspapers piled on the sideboard. The only person in the room was a gentleman sitting at one of the tables reading a newspaper. He was clean shaven, with a neat brown moustache. He wore a colourful black and red vest, and a black tie knotted at his throat. *That's Mr. Little*, I thought, *ready to greet the tavern's guests.*

"Mr. Little?" I pulled my letter of introduction from my pocket.

He looked up from his newspaper. "I am he. And you, I presume, are Dory Dickson."

I was speechless with surprise that he knew my name. He laughed, "Ho, ho, ho! I didn't mean to startle you. In Morpeth we have postal service three times a week. Sam Kemp wrote to me about you and your journey." He waved away the letter of introduction that I held out to him. "I expected you ten days ago. What held you up?"

"My horse went lame."

"Ah! Horses do that, especially when you need them to be sound. Well, take your horse to the stable. I believe you have a sled carrying a valuable load. Is it well covered?"

"With a heavy tarpaulin, securely tied down."

"I don't suppose any harm can come to it outdoors, but tell the stable hand to haul the sled into the drive shed, just to be sure. When you've looked after the horse and sled, I'll see you back here."

The stable hand gave Labelle a stall. I rubbed her down, checked her feet—all were fine—and fed and watered her myself. When I returned to the tavern, Mr. Little was no longer alone. A man with sandy hair and reddish whiskers had joined him. I stopped in the doorway and looked at him. Could that be Duncan Fraser? The two men were seated at the table, chatting and drinking coffee. As soon as I heard the newcomer's voice with its Scottish burr, I knew it was.

"Hello!" I exclaimed, and I rushed up to shake his hand. But he didn't greet me as a friend. Remaining seated, he looked at me as if I were a stranger. Then he said, "Aren't you the lad who looks after the fires at the tavern in Chippawa?"

I could hardly believe my ears. Why was Duncan pretending not to know me? And what was he doing here? I stood there dumb as a post, puzzled what it all meant. But it didn't take me long to guess. Duncan had told me he travelled all over the country for Hunters' Lodge meetings. I figured there was going to be a meeting right here at this tavern, and he didn't want Mr. Little to become suspicious.

I said simply, "That's me. I cut wood and look after the fires."

"So what are you doing here?"

Of course, Duncan knew perfectly well. After all, Morpeth was on the Talbot Road, directly on the way to Jacob Fox's farm. But if Duncan didn't want to raise Mr. Little's suspicions, I was ready to play the same game. I told Duncan about the loom and spinning wheel I was taking to Mrs. Fox. Mr. Little listened quietly, a slightly amused expression on his face, while I explained all this to Duncan.

"When did you leave Chippawa?" Duncan again feigned ignorance.

"The thirtieth of December—the day after the *Caroline* was cut loose and burned."

As soon as I mentioned the *Caroline*, Mr. Little spoke up, "It must have been an amazing sight—a blazing ship going over Niagara Falls."

Duncan laughed, "That story is already becoming a legend. Like most legends, it isn't completely true. The ship was blazing while she drifted down the Niagara River. She was blazing when she stranded in a bed of reeds. After that, she came loose and kept on drifting. The fire burned out, and she sank without ever reaching the falls. I believe some pieces may have gone over the brink, but they weren't burning when they did."

"Too bad," said Mr. Little. "A blazing ship plunging over Niagara Falls makes a better story."

"Ach, that's true," said Duncan. "But the spectacle isn't important. What matters is the result. The loss of the *Caroline* forced William Lyon Mackenzie to evacuate Navy Island. On January the fourteenth, he took away his army and all the weapons he had collected there."

This was news to me. What else had happened during the quiet days I was housebound with Ralph and Miranda?

Mr. Little now appeared to notice that I was still standing there, wearing my outdoor clothes. "Take off your coat and hat and pull up a chair," he said kindly. He picked up a small brass bell from the table. At his ring, a girl wearing a white apron and a little white cap came from a back room, which I supposed was the kitchen. Mr. Little sent her to bring me coffee and a few biscuits. I set my bundle on the floor and, after taking off my hat, coat and scarf, sat down with Mr. Little and Duncan.

Duncan waited while the girl arrived with my coffee and some sweet biscuits. When she had left, he continued, "The burning of the *Caroline* was an act of war. President Van Buran doesn't want war with Britain. But he had to do something. So he sent General Winfield Scott to the Niagara frontier to protect American interests. That made things too hot for Mackenzie. He ordered all the arms and munitions that he had collected on Navy Island to be placed on board a steamer, the *Barcelona*, to be taken upriver and unloaded on the American side.

"But Captain Andrew Drew—the same officer who'd led the party that cut loose and burned the *Caroline*—got wind of this. To be ready to intercept the *Barcelona*, he had two Canadian gunboats moored at the head of Grand Island a couple of miles upriver, lying in wait.

"General Scott learned about the gunboats. He didn't want the *Barcelona* to meet the same fate as the *Caroline*. So he placed a battery of artillery on the American shore and warned Captain Drew that if the Canadian ships attacked the *Barcelona*, he would blow them out of the water.

"Knowing that General Scott could and would do exactly that, Captain Drew backed off and let the *Barcelona* proceed unmolested. Her freight was unloaded on the American shore of Lake Erie. From there it's being carried to homes of sympathizers, who will keep it hidden in their cellars and barns."

"What about Mackenzie's army?" I asked. "He had four hundred men on Navy Island, training to invade Canada."

"They'll strike somewhere else."

Duncan had now said all that he was going to say. When I had finished my coffee and biscuits, Mr. Little summoned the serving girl again. He told her to put me in one of the back bedrooms overlooking the stable yard and be sure I got a good dinner and breakfast in the morning.

The girl waited while I gathered up my bundle, my scarf and my coat and hat. Then she led me up a flight of stairs to a small bedroom, simply furnished with a four-poster bed, a wardrobe and a chair. When she lad left, I sat on the chair wondering what to do with the rest of the day. If it hadn't been cold and cloudy outdoors, I might have gone for a walk around town. On the other hand, I liked the idea of relaxing in the public room and maybe reading one of those newspapers I'd seen piled on the sideboard. So I combed my hair to make myself presentable and went back to the public room.

Duncan was no longer there, and Mr. Little was busy chatting with a guest who had just arrived. I walked over to the sideboard to look at the newspapers. There were three or four copies of *The Constitution* and about the same number of copies of another newspaper called the *Upper Canada Gazette.* They were all of different dates. I thought I'd start with *The Constitution* because that was the newspaper I'd seen Duncan reading in his room at Mr. Kemp's tavern in Chippawa.

I carried it over to one of the little tables and sat down to read it. Right away I saw that this was going to be hard work. There were seven narrow columns all squeezed together on the front page, with hardly any space between the columns, and not a single picture to look at. The first story I read praised the French system of government and the United States system of government. According to the writer, if we wanted to enjoy the liberty and equality the French and the Americans enjoyed, our first step was to rid ourselves of the monarchy. That was exactly what Duncan had told me. Then we had to reform society by making everyone equal. It might take a revolution to do that, because the corrupt, greedy ruling class had everything arranged for their own benefit rather than for the benefit of all the people. In another story, I read that William Lyon Mackenzie's Committee of Grievances had submitted a report 570 pages long to the British government, and now Lieutenant Governor Sir Francis Bond Head was about to be replaced because of his failure to deal with all the problems.

I read *The Constitution* for a full hour before my eyes hurt and the words began to blur together. All that reading made me hungry. The next time the serving girl came into the public room, I caught her eye. When she came over to my table, I asked her if she could bring me some supper. She smiled and said Yes. After waiting on two gentlemen whom I took to be paying guests, she brought me a plate loaded with roast beef, mashed turnips and potatoes. When I had finished that, she served me a piece of apple pie and a cup of tea. This nourishment set me up to have a look at the other newspaper, the *Upper Canada Gazette*.

It was as different from *The Constitution* as night from day. According to the *Upper Canada Gazette,* the grievances in Mackenzie's report—all 570 pages of them—were a hoax. They existed only in the fevered brains of radical Reformers. Unfortunately, these scoundrels had hoodwinked his Gracious Majesty King William, and now our Sovereign Lady Queen Victoria, into launching an investigation, which could have no other effect than to threaten good government and political stability in the Province of Upper Canada. As for equality, that was forever an impossibility, because all men were *not* created equal, never had been and never would be.

Reading this, I'd had enough. I folded the *Upper Canada Gazette* and returned it to the stack of newspapers on the sideboard. Outside, darkness had fallen. The clock on the fireplace mantelpiece told me it was only eight o'clock, but I was ready to turn in for the night as soon as I had been out to the stable to check Labelle's' foot and make sure she was comfortable in her stall.

CHAPTER SIXTEEN

I came down to breakfast next morning to find Duncan Fraser sitting at one of the tables in the public room, eating a plateful of bacon and eggs. His reddish whiskers were neatly trimmed, and he looked ready to start the day. From the way he glanced at me, one eyebrow raised, I had the feeling that he had been lying in wait for me to enter.

"Come join me, Laddie," he said. I sat down at his table. He gave me a keen look. "I thought we might have a talk before you go on your way."

"What kind of talk?" I asked.

I suspected that I was in for one of Duncan's lectures about the Family Compact—not that I disagreed with his views, especially after reading those newspapers. But I didn't want Canada to become a republic, and I didn't like the way Duncan asked for help from Americans. The Family Compact was our problem, for the people of Upper Canada to solve. I didn't want a lecture, but I did want an explanation why he had pretended not to know me.

The serving girl came out from the kitchen just then to ask what I wanted for breakfast, I told her I wanted bacon and eggs, same as Duncan had. As soon as she had gone back to the kitchen, I asked him straight out to tell me the reason.

"A necessary precaution," he answered. "The fewer people who know a secret, the safer it is for everybody."

I shook my head. "I don't have any secrets."

"You may not think so." He took a bite of bacon, chewed thoughtfully, and then he said. "Sam Kemp gave you a list of names of people who'd help you. Let me see it."

"No!"

"Why not?"

"I gave Mr. Kemp my solemn word that no other eyes than mine will ever see the list."

"Exactly! I won't pry or urge you to break your promise, but I'll wager that some people on his list support the Family Compact, some support the Patriots and some stay completely out of politics. All they have in common is that they're Sam Kemp's friends . . . or they owe him a favour. That list will be made up of different people with very different views. But if it falls into the wrong hands, all will be tarred with the same brush. Keeping it secret protects everyone on the list."

I thought this over. The list *was* made up of an odd mixture of people, some with opposing views. Of course, Mr. Kemp would not want to cause trouble for any of them. "That's right," I said. "Now may I ask you a question?"

"Of course, Laddie. Ask away. But that doesn't mean I'll answer it."

"Did you come to Morpeth for a meeting of the Hunters' Lodge?"

His eyes narrowed. After a moment he said, "Yes."

"Last night, did the Hunters' Lodge meet here, the same as you met at Mr. Kemp's tavern in Chippawa?"

"Ach, that's a secret I don't want to give away. Any more questions?"

"Just one more. The night we saw the *Caroline* burning, you said, 'This will change everything.' When I left to join the others in the public room, you stayed in your room with the door closed because you wanted to keep out of the way until things settled down. That's what you said."

"You have a good memory, Dory."

"Now you tell us that William Lyon Mackenzie has moved his army away from Navy Island. Four hundred men. Where did they go?"

"Some to Michigan. Some to Ohio. Different places."

"My father warned me to avoid border towns because of Patriots causing trouble. He told me that the settlements along the Talbot Road were good places for me to look for work. But here you are . . ."

"You mean, causing trouble?"

"I don't mean *you* cause trouble. But there seems to be trouble wherever you are."

The girl brought my breakfast. Duncan waited until she had gone. Then he said, "I've been visiting many places along the Talbot Road. Not just for meetings of the Hunters' Lodge, but for talk with ordinary people. I can tell you that thousands of men—farmers, tradesmen, shopkeepers, teachers—will join the Patriots if there's an invasion of Canada. Do you wonder at that? Canadians look across the border and see the liberty and equality that folks have in the United States. With Americans' support, we can have the same in Canada."

I picked up my knife and fork. While I was cutting my bacon into little pieces, I said, "I think the Americans just want to annex Canada and make it part of the United States."

"Some do. Some don't. We have to take a chance. Revolution is coming. Blood will be shed. It's like treating an illness. When you're sick, the doctor opens a vein in your arm and draws out a pint of blood. Bloodletting is part of the cure."

I loaded my fork with bacon and egg. Before lifting it to my mouth, I said, "If the doctor's knife slips, his patient may die from loss of blood."

Duncan raised one shoulder and let it fall. "That's a risk he has to take."

After that, he gave his attention to his breakfast, as I did to mine. I sensed that more than just our conversation had come to an end. We finished eating in silence. Duncan wished me a safe journey when we parted. There was disappointment in his sharp blue eyes.

Travelling west, I made good progress that day. It was cold, January weather, the fields white and the sun glinting off the snow-covered roofs of houses and barns. The country was flat.

I could see for miles, except there was nothing interesting to see. That night I stayed at the home of a farmer. He and his wife had about a dozen children of different sizes, some of them twins. I couldn't figure out what connection the farmer had to Mr. Kemp. He asked me a lot of questions about where I came from and what crops we grew on our farm. I told him the whole sad story about the harvest failing and both our cow and our horse dying the same year. I didn't mention the Family Compact, and neither did he. The next morning I set out again.

For two more days the bright weather continued. On the morning of the third day, a sign nailed to a post told me that we were now in Gosfield Township. Soon we would reach Jacob Fox's farm.

CHAPTER SEVENTEEN

he day began clear, but around noon the sky darkened and a wind sprang up in the west. Its gusts whipped up the snow. We were in for a blizzard. I hoped to reach Jacob Fox's farm before it arrived. But luck was against us. Soon driving snow lashed my face. By the middle of the afternoon, houses, barns and trees were all disappearing and I could no longer see any dividing line between earth and sky. There were only two things that kept us on the road. The first was Labelle's unerring sense for where to put her next foot forward. The other was my occasional glimpse of the top rail of a snake fence separating a farmer's field from the road.

Mr. Kemp's directions were clear. I was looking for Lot 24, the farm of Jacob Fox.

Labelle ploughed gamely ahead. Finally, through the swirling snow I saw a sign with the name JACOB FOX painted on a board. The board was nailed to a post that marked the entrance to a lane.

"Gee!" I shouted, telling Labelle to turn right. The lane led to a small log cabin that had a larger log addition built onto it, the two joined together to make one good-size house. Only the smaller section had a front door.

I stepped down from the sled and trudged to the door, which was painted black and had iron strap hinges that reached nearly across its full width. I knocked hard. After a moment, a man came to the door. He was tall and big-shouldered, with a farmer's tanned, weathered face.

"Good day," I said. "I'm looking for Jacob Fox. Or, I should say, I'm looking for Mrs. Elizabeth Fox. My name is Theodore Dickson, known as Dory. I've come from Chippawa—"

He did not wait to hear more. Instead of inviting me to come in, the man stepped outside into the driving snow and closed the door behind him. Standing there in his shirtsleeves, he said, "I'm Jacob Fox. I've been waiting two weeks for you."

Waiting two weeks for me? This must mean that Mr. Kemp had written a letter to tell Mrs. Fox about the loom and spinning wheel. But why should her husband feel such urgency about my arrival? It made no sense.

I started to explain my delay. "My horse went lame—"

"Never mind!" He interrupted me. "We'll take your sled to the old barn. That's the safest place."

Why did he care about safety? My confusion grew. "What's the danger?" I asked.

Without explaining, he made a dash through the swirling snow to Labelle and grabbed her bridle. His hands were big-knuckled, large and powerful. He looked back at me, where I was still standing on his doorstep.

"Come on! What are you waiting for?" He had a deep, commanding voice. Labelle did not like this rough stranger grabbing her bridle. She laid her ears back, whinnied and tossed her head. I didn't like it either.

"I'll lead her!" I protested. I ran to my horse and snatched the bridle from his hand.

Labelle and I followed Jacob Fox through the blizzard to the yard behind the house. There were two barns, a large, new-looking frame barn and a small, dilapidated log barn, which was the one he led me to. The door was padlocked. He reached into his trousers' pocket, pulled out a ring of keys, and undid the lock. The old door sagged on its hinges, so that it took both of us to open it. As soon as we had Labelle and the sled inside, he pulled the door shut.

The barn was empty except for a stack of lumber and a heap of tools. Without taking time to unhitch the sled, Jacob picked up a metal bar. "Let's have a look at these guns," he muttered as he set to work pulling out the bolts that fastened the tarpaulin to the floorboards of the sled.

"There's been a mistake!" I pawed at his arm, trying to stop him. "There are no guns. I've brought a loom and a spinning wheel for Mrs. Fox! They belonged to Mrs. Kemp. It was her dying wish that your wife should have them." Jacob paid me no heed, wrenching out bolts one after another. Pop! Pop! Pop!

He grunted as he worked. "No need to keep up the show. We both know what this is and who it's for." By now he had the bolts removed along the front edge and one side. Bracing his feet for a great effort, he threw back the tarpaulin.

I gasped. In front of me, stacked and tied down, were enough muskets to arm a regiment. He saw the look on my face. "Good Lord!" he exclaimed. "Did you really expect to see a loom and a spinning wheel?"

I nodded, dumb with shock. At last I managed to say, "Does Mr. Kemp know his sled was loaded with muskets and not with a loom and spinning wheel?"

Jacob Fox smiled. "I daresay he can tell the difference."

"Where did they come from?"

"American sympathizers stole these guns from the armory in Buffalo and smuggled them across the border to Chippawa. The plan was to ferry them over to Mackenzie's headquarters on Navy Island. Sam Kemp was storing them while waiting for a chance to do that. The burning of the *Caroline* changed the plan. In just one night, Sam's shed in Chippawa became too close for comfort. He had to get rid of forty muskets as fast as he could."

"But . . . but . . . Mr. Kemp isn't helping the Patriots. He doesn't take sides."

"Of course he can't take sides. Sam wouldn't be half as useful if he did."

Mr. Kemp useful to the Patriots! It was like an ice jam bursting in my brain. Suddenly everything made sense. I had wondered if Mr. Kemp knew about the Hunters' Lodge meeting in his tavern. Of course he knew! He too was part of the conspiracy to overthrow the government of Upper Canada.

"He didn't tell me they were guns," I said lamely. I stood there staring at the muskets, with their wooden stocks and long barrels. From the shape of the load under the tarpaulin, Miranda had thought it looked like firewood. Old Mrs. Hoover in Williamsville had been surprised to hear that that her niece Mrs. Kemp owned a loom and spinning wheel. The truth was, she didn't. The loom and spinning wheel did not exist. They were just a lie.

"The fewer people who know a secret," said Jacob Fox, "the fewer there are to let it slip." These words startled me, for they were almost the same words that I had heard from Duncan Fraser at the tavern in Morpeth.

"Why bring the muskets all this distance?" I asked. "I've hauled them two hundred miles. Mr. Kemp could have sent them somewhere much closer to Chippawa to be hidden."

"He sent them here because this is the closest place to Pelee Island along the entire north shore of Lake Erie. These muskets will be needed there very soon. We have plenty of ammunition stored on Pelee Island, but not enough guns."

Pelee Island. I recalled Ralph Butler's words: "It's a very peaceful place, but that's likely to change." There were rumours, Ralph had told me, that William Lyon Mackenzie's Patriots planned to take over Pelee Island as the first step to invading Canada. So the rumours were true. And I was the one who brought the guns. At that moment, I wanted the ground to open up under my feet and swallow me.

"Now," said Jacob Fox, "I'll refasten these bolts and we'll get your horse into a stall in the new barn. Then you can meet my family." He paused and looked at me, his head to one side. "We need an excuse for you coming here."

"What?" I was so confused that I couldn't think straight about anything.

"How old are you?"

"Fourteen."

"How long have you been working for Sam Kemp?"

"Only two days, before he sent me here."

"Hm." Jacob appeared to think things over. Finally he said. "Sam must trust you, to send you all the way from Chippawa." Abruptly, he made up his mind. "Look. I'll say you're a friend of Sam's family—no, a relative. You can say that you're looking for a chance to better yourself and Sam thinks you have better prospects around here than in Niagara. That will explain why you're going to stay with us for the next few weeks."

It sounded like a good excuse. But why should I stay more than one night? As soon as I'd rested my horse and had a good sleep, I'd be ready to leave.

Jacob laid his powerful hand on my shoulder. "Not one word about looms, spinning wheels or muskets. This," he pointed to the load of guns, "is not something for women and children to know about. It's men's business."

Despite my confusion, I felt a flush of pride that he regarded me as a man, not as a child.

CHAPTER EIGHTEEN

The new barn housed two horses, six cows, a bull and a huge pregnant sow that looked ready to drop her piglets any day now. We put Labelle into a stall and fed and watered her. When we left the barn, the storm still raged. It was cold outside, and it had been cold in both barns. Jacob Fox, in his shirtsleeves, did not appear to notice the temperature. I thought, *The man must be made of iron!*

From the barnyard, the back door opened directly onto the kitchen. As soon as the door was shut, I set down my bundle against the wall, took off my snow-crusted hat, scarf and coat, and hung them on a hook. The kitchen was a large room with a big cast-iron stove and a wooden table long enough to seat a dozen people. Against one wall stood a tall sideboard, which had china plates ranged on its open shelves. Every plate had a rose painted on it. The roses were pink and yellow with green leaves.

Jacob noticed me looking around. "This kitchen was the entire original cabin," he said. "Now we use it just for cooking and eating. The new addition is our sitting room." He waved his hand in the direction of a closed door, through which I heard women's voices. "I'll take you there to meet the family. Just remember: no talk about looms, spinning wheels or guns."

I tugged my fingers through my messy hair, wishing I had time to get my comb from my bundle. Jacob opened the door and motioned me to enter ahead of him. The people in the sitting room all looked up.

"This is Dory Dickson," said Jacob. "He just arrived from Chippawa." Nobody looked surprised to have a guest presented to them in this manner, brought in out of a blizzard. "Dory is kin to our friend Sam Kemp. He's going to stay with us for a while."

Jacob Fox now introduced his family, beginning with his wife Elizabeth, to whom I had expected to deliver a spinning wheel and a loom. She was sitting in a rocking chair by the fire, knitting a sock. On being introduced, she stood up, causing a ball of wool to roll off her lap onto the floor. "You're very welcome," she said. Then she picked up the ball of wool and sat down again. The fire was invitingly bright and warm.

"The wife and I have nine children," said Jacob. "The four oldest have grown up and moved away. Just five still live at home." He waved his hand toward a girl sitting on a sofa, an embroidery frame in her hands. "That's Sarah, my old-maid daughter."

Sarah protested. "Vati, I'm just eighteen—hardly an old maid yet!" Sarah was very pretty, with ivory skin and dark curls that covered her neck. In my opinion, she didn't need to stay an old maid one day longer than she wished to.

Then came Anna, who was close to my age. She had light brown hair, parted in the middle and braided smoothly, and large brown eyes. She was seated at a small table, on which a book lay open. Anna's face was too solemn and serious to call pretty, but I liked the look of her.

Finally, Jacob introduced the boys. William was about eleven years old, George around seven, and Peter no more than five—the same as my little sister Susan. All three were crouched on a braided rug on the floor, gathered around a checkerboard. William was watching his older brothers play. The boys looked up and said hello, and then they returned to their game. All the children called Jacob Fox 'Vati'. I supposed it meant Pa or Father in some other language, although the family spoke English the same as I did.

"How is Mr. Kemp managing?" Mrs. Fox asked me. "It's been six months since he lost his wife."

"He's very well."

"I was saddened to learn of Mrs. Kemp's death. But now she is in a better place." Elizabeth Fox's knitting needles clicked for a minute before she asked, "Had she been ill for a long time?"

I had no idea how to answer this question. "Not very long." I tried in vain to think of something comforting to add.

"She was a dear friend of mine. I wish I had a keepsake to remember her by."

Seeing a tear on her cheek, I felt sorry that the loom and spinning wheel had been only a story. Mrs. Fox said no more as she continued her knitting.

There was an empty chair at the table where Anna was sitting, so I sat down across from her. She asked why I had chosen the very dead of winter to travel. Not sure how to answer this question either, I mumbled that maybe I'd look for work in this area. Standing by the fireplace, Jacob Fox regarded me sternly. He may have been afraid that I would blurt something about muskets, but I kept my mouth shut.

"Dory's going to stay with us for a few weeks," Jacob said. "He can sleep up in the loft with William, George and Peter."

I was glad to know that I'd have someplace to sleep. But why did he want me to stay so long? One night would be enough. Mr. Kemp needed me at the tavern. But I could explain this in the morning. For the moment, I was ready to relax.

The sitting room was cozy and warm. It had plank walls, hiding the logs underneath. Hanging on one wall were framed samplers of needlework, the sort that girls do when they're about twelve years old to show off their stitches. There were four samplers. Each displayed the letters of the alphabet, a picture and a motto carefully embroidered. The samplers were signed and dated. Anna's sampler (1836) had a picture of a man giving an apple to a lady, along with a poem:

Who has a friend
With whom to share
Has double cheer
And half the care.

"That's a beautiful poem," I said to Anna. "Did you make it up?"

An amused smile lifted the corners of her mouth. "No. I didn't write that poem. But I do love poetry." So we talked about poetry, which meant that I listened to her talk. She said that she liked the poetry of Shelley and Lord Byron, although they led scandalous lives. I was curious to know more about this, but she blushed and refused to explain.

"What's that book you're reading now?" I pointed to the book lying open in front of her.

"It's *Gulliver's Travels.*"

"I've read it."

Her eyes opened wide. "Are you book-learned?"

"I haven't had much chance to be book-learned. We have no books at home. But when I was still at school the schoolmaster loaned his own books to any pupil who showed an interest. I borrowed two from him: *Robinson Crusoe* and *Gulliver's Travels.*"

I would have liked to talk with Anna longer, but Mrs. Fox put her knitting away and said to Sarah and Anna, "Come, girls. It's time to make dinner."

No sooner had they left the room, than Jacob sent the three boys out to the barn to tend to the livestock. Now that he and I were alone, he wasted no time getting down to business.

"Dory, here's the situation. Over in Ohio, at Sandusky, there's an army getting ready to invade Pelee Island. It's not a regular army. The United States has a treaty of neutrality with Great Britain. President Van Buren doesn't want war. So this army is neither legal nor professional, although some of its leaders are experienced military men."

"What's the point of an army from Sandusky invading Pelee

Island if the American government doesn't want a war?"

"There's reason to believe that thousands of ordinary Canadians are just waiting for a chance to break away from England and make Canada a republic. These American volunteers want to help."

"I've heard that before," I said, recalling what Duncan Fraser had told me the night I stayed at the tavern in Morpeth.

"Sam Kemp wrote to tell me that you were bringing forty muskets, though he didn't say this in so many words. I had to read between the lines. You can never be sure a letter won't fall into the wrong hands. Anyway, I didn't understand from his letter that he was keeping you in the dark. Now that I think about it, I know why. On your way here, there must have been occasions when you might have let something slip."

"I've brought you the muskets. My work is done. What I know or don't know doesn't matter."

"Not so fast. Your work is not done. You'll be staying here until the ice on Lake Erie is strong enough. Then you are going to take those muskets over to Pelee Island."

CHAPTER NINETEEN

hen Jacob Fox told me I was going to take those muskets over to Pelee Island, I had my answer ready. "Sir, I can't do that. Mr. Kemp expects me back in Chippawa. He's been without the horse and sled for three weeks, and he needs me at the tavern to keep the fires burning."

"I've written to Sam," Jacob said in his commanding voice. "I told him I'm keeping you here until the ice is strong enough for you to take the muskets over to Pelee Island. As for your work at his tavern, there's always some fellow he can hire to keep the fires burning."

"I've never driven a sled over ice. I've no experience."

"Not necessary."

"To speak frankly, Sir, I don't want to take the muskets to Pelee Island."

"It doesn't matter what you want."

Nothing was left but to speak the truth. "Mr. Fox, I know we need reform in Upper Canada. But there must be a peaceful way to bring about change. Fighting isn't the only way."

His face grew hard. "It's all settled."

"But—"

I had no chance to say more. At that moment Sarah opened the door from the kitchen to announce that dinner was ready. When Jacob and I entered the kitchen, the rest of the family were already seated at the long table. My chair was pointed out. I sat down and, like the others, bowed my head while Jacob gave the blessing over the food.

After dinner, the womenfolk washed the dishes. Then Mrs. Fox brought out a deck of cards. "Do you know how to play whist?" she asked.

"No, ma'am."

"Then you must learn."

Apart from her sadness at the death of her friend, you'd think she didn't have a care in the world. But then, she didn't know about the muskets. Neither did Sarah or Anna or the boys. I supposed they were all the happier for not knowing that the head of their family was involved in a plot to overthrow the government of Upper Canada.

"I'll be your partner," said Anna.

We settled down to play whist, Anna and I against Mrs. Fox and Sarah. Although Mrs. Fox carefully explained the rules of the game, my mind was too preoccupied to keep track of the cards. We played for an hour. While we played, Jacob Fox sat in an armchair by the fire, reading his newspaper and puffing on his pipe. He looked at me from time to time, and I felt his stern eyes examining me.

Anna and I lost the game. This was mostly my fault, but she didn't seem to mind. Mrs. Fox gave me a candle to light my way up the steep, narrow stairs to the loft, which was a large room above the kitchen. The metal stove pipe from the woodstove ran up through a hole in the ceiling to warm the loft.

Little Peter was sound asleep, but William and George were still awake. There were two unoccupied beds in the loft. "Take either of those beds," William told me. "They belonged to our older brothers, but they've moved away."

"Thanks." I chose the bed that was the further away from William and George so I wouldn't seem to be listening in on their conversation. I took off my boots, shirt and trousers, blew out my candle and climbed into bed. After a few minutes, the boys stopped talking.

In the darkness of the loft, I imagined that I saw the stack of muskets tied down to the floor of the sled. I drew the blanket over my head and tried to think of something else. But with the wind howling about the eaves and the snow lashing the loft window and the storm in my mind raging as fiercely as the blizzard outdoors, it was late when I fell asleep.

In the morning the storm was over. Jacob Fox took me down to the shore to check the progress of the freeze-up. Although the ice on the lake extended for miles, it did not touch the shore.

Between the solid ice sheet and the shore lay a six-foot gap filled with slush. The slush made a musical, rustling sound as it lapped upon the beach. In the far distance steam was rising. Jacob raised his arm and pointed toward the steam. "Where you see mist, that's open water."

I peered into the distance. "Can I see Pelee Island from here?"

"No. Pelee Island is twenty miles due south. You won't be able to see it until you're halfway across. Then you'll see the lighthouse on a point at the northeast corner of the island."

"I've heard about the lighthouse," I said. "A man who grew up on Pelee Island told me about all the shipwrecks before the lighthouse was built. I stayed with him and his wife for more than a week when my horse went lame."

"The Pelee Passage is a treacherous stretch of water," said Jacob. "Shoals, reefs, strong currents. Even in winter, the water keeps moving under the ice. Pressure builds up. I wouldn't send you out on it now. We need a few really cold nights before the ice will be strong enough for a sled loaded with muskets to cross safely."

I was glad to hear this and welcomed the delay, because I still hoped for a way to avoid taking those guns to Pelee Island.

During the weeks while we waited, I spent most of my days chopping wood and splitting kindling. In the evenings we played whist. Everyone in the family had work to do, and I was treated like one of the family. Jacob Fox let me drive his sleigh, which was the low-slung kind called a Canadian cariole. On Sunday afternoons I took Anna and Sarah for sleigh rides. Essex County is absolutely flat, not a hill in sight. I would put Labelle into a brisk trot, and we'd speed along the snow-packed Talbot Road, sleigh bells jingling. If it had not been for dread of the unwelcome journey that lay ahead, those days would have been among the happiest of my life.

In mid-February there was a cold snap that lasted several days. Steam stopped rising from the lake. The slushy gap between the shore and the ice sheet froze solid. Lying awake at night, I listened to the ice on the lake creak and boom and groan.

Late one afternoon as I stood on the shore with Jacob Fox, we saw a number of tiny black dots far out on the ice. In a little while, the dots grew to the size of ants. They were moving toward us. Soon it was clear that dozens of horse-drawn sleighs, spread out over the ice, were heading in our direction.

"I'll fetch my spyglass," Jacob said. He went back to the house. When he returned, he put the spyglass to his eye. "Just as I thought. It's the McCormicks, and not only William and his family. It looks like their servants and farmhands are with them . . . other families, too. Probably they're McCormick's tenants. All of them are scared for their lives, I suppose."

As they came closer, the sleighs veered west. "They're going to Colchester," Jacob said, "The McCormick family has a home there. McCormicks have been settled in Colchester for generations."

He handed his spyglass to me. When I had the lens adjusted, I saw that the sleighs were packed with people. Jacob's deep voice was at my ear. "William McCormick must have received a warning that the invasion is coming soon. That means we have no time to waste. We must get those muskets over to Pelee Island as fast as we can. The Patriot army will need them.

"Here's what we have to do. Tonight you wait in bed until the boys are asleep, and then you come down from the loft. Sleep on the sofa in the sitting room. I'll get everything ready and waken you about six o'clock before the rest of the family is stirring."

He pointed south across the frozen lake. "Your horse can cover that distance in half a day. When you start out, it will still be dark, though some light will be showing in the east. Keep the sunrise on your left. By daybreak you'll be able to see the Pelee Island lighthouse. You must go ashore at the northwest corner of the island. There you'll find a road that leads south. Follow that road right to the end. Watch for Adam Bruner's place. That's where you'll deliver the muskets. You'll see Bruner's name on a sign nailed to his fence post."

Jacob Fox's directions were coming at me too fast. I must have looked just as stunned as I felt, because he stopped talking and laid his hand on my shoulder. "Don't worry. You can't get lost on an island that's nine miles long by four miles wide. Anyway, I'll draw you a map."

CHAPTER TWENTY

A restless night I had of it. With the fire banked, the sitting room was cold. The only sound was the creaking of the ice on the lake—the twenty miles of bleak, barren ice that I must cross with the sled load of muskets. It was still dark when Jacob Fox roused me at six o'clock. I had not undressed, so all I had to put on were my outer clothes: my coat, my boots, my coonskin hat and my long knitted scarf. I wrapped the scarf around my neck right up to my ears.

I went outside with Jacob. While I was still sleeping, he had dragged the loaded sled out of the old log barn. He had the bolts tight, the tarpaulin securely fastened, and Labelle already hitched up and ready to go. He handed me a sheet of paper.

"Here's the map I drew."

I studied it by the light of his lantern. The map showed a long point of land, identified as Point Pelee, reaching south into Lake Erie from the mainland. Beyond it was Pelee Island, and then there were some other islands and a stretch of water labelled 'The Pelee Passage.' The sketch of Pelee Island showed the lighthouse at the northeast point. It marked the spot where I should go ashore at the northwest tip, as well as the road that led south along the island's western shore. Adam Bruner's place at the southwest point was marked with an X.

"Everything's ready if you are," he said.

"I'm ready." My voice was calm, but my heart thudded in my chest.

"One final word." Jacob was standing with his hand on Labelle's bridle. "I have three brothers who live on Pelee Island.,

George, John and Henry. They don't support the rebellion. I've done my best to recruit them, but they won't budge from their allegiance to the Crown. Still, despite our differences, they are my brothers. When the invasion comes, the Patriot army will not molest them. Their leaders have given their solemn word not to harm them or their property. My brothers know about this promise. That's the reason they haven't fled from the island, as many others have done." He cleared his throat nervously. "I don't expect you'll meet my brothers, but I thought I should let you know."

He took from his belt a large knife. "Take this." The blade glinted in the light of the lantern. "I've honed the edge sharp as a razor."

"What's it for?"

"In case you need to cut the traces . . ."

So he too was worried about the ice. Though not in so many words, he was telling me that in an emergency I should sever the side straps by which Labelle pulled the sled. In order to save her, I should let the sled and its load go to the bottom of the lake.

"Thank you." I didn't have a sheath or a belt to stick the knife into. So I laid it on the sled floor under my seat, where it would be easy to grab if needed.

Jacob cleared his throat again. "When you've unloaded the sled at Adam Bruner's place, rest your horse for a couple of hours and then come straight back here. Without the weight of the muskets, you'll make good time." His voice had a note of forced confidence. "You'll be back before midnight. I'll be watching for you." I climbed onto my seat on the sled and picked up the reins. Jacob said, "McCormick's people all got safely across the ice, so you will too."

"I'm not worried," I said a little too loudly.

"Safe journey!" He went back to the house. The light of his lantern receded and then disappeared. I waited for a moment, feeling scared and alone. Then Labelle gave her harness a shake, eager to start moving. I said to myself, *The sooner I'm*

rid of these muskets, the sooner I can put all this behind me. So
I gave a slap of the reins. The clip-clop of Labelle's hooves on
the hard-packed snow was the only sound as we made on our
way down the lane and across the road to the Lake Erie shore.
Labelle paused at the edge, lowered her head and sniffed at
the frozen expanse ahead of her.

"Get up, Labelle!" At my urging, she stepped onto the ice.
The night was as black as the grave. Not a glimpse of moon-
shine pierced the thick blanket of cloud. When I turned my
head to look back; darkness hid the mainland from my sight.
I saw no sign yet of the dawning light in the east that was to
guide me. Labelle kept moving, her hooves clicking on the ice.
It felt eerie and mysterious to be out there on the vast, frozen
lake. I did not trust the ice. The only thing I trusted was my
horse. She, I suspected, felt the same about me.

CHAPTER TWENTY-ONE

e were about a mile out from shore before I saw in the east the faint grey light of dawn. Soon after, I glimpsed the long, low stretch of Point Pelee projecting southward from the mainland. Jacob Fox had told me that as soon as I came even with the tip of Point Pelee, I'd see Pelee Island straight ahead. If it were summer, I'd have the light from the Pelee Island lighthouse to guide me. But in winter the lamps in the lantern remained unlit.

By the time we had covered ten or so miles, the sun had risen and the clouds had cleared away. The space of the sky above was vast, and the expanse of frozen water was vast. Three times I heard the ice crack close by. I slapped the reins and called to Labelle to quicken her pace. Every step would bring us closer to solid land.

In the distance I saw a place where steam was rising. Open water. This was unexpected. But the mist was far away to the southeast, not due south the way I was heading. On the horizon, I saw a white dot straight ahead. A little further on, the white dot took shape as the Pelee Island lighthouse. *It looks just like its picture in Ralph Butler's painting,* I said to myself. The tower was tall and white, with a slight lean to the southwest. Early morning sunshine glinted on the lantern windows at the top. Seeing the lighthouse made me feel safe.

I pulled out the map. There was the lighthouse standing at the tip of Brushy Marsh Point at the northeast tip of the island. I knew I had to keep to the right of the lighthouse in order to be sure I went ashore at the northwest point. That's where I would find the start of the road that would take me to Adam Bruner's place at the southwest tip of Pelee Island.

All was going well until we were half a mile from Pelee Island's northwest point. That was when I noticed water an inch deep overflowing the ice. Labelle had been trotting briskly. I slowed her to a walk. We had to advance carefully, because the ice was beginning to go up and down under her hooves. I thought about the weight of the sled, with its heavy load of muskets. Reaching under my seat, I picked up the knife Jacob had given me to use in case it became necessary to cut the traces to free my horse. I was sweating, despite the cold.

"Go on! Go on!" I called to Labelle. She strained forward at every step. We were about one hundred yards from shore when suddenly she stopped moving. She lowered her head. This time I did not urge her on but left the sled and stumbled forward. Labelle whinnied at the touch of my hand upon her neck. Before us lay a wide crack in the ice, revealing a strip of dark water two feet wide. I could jump across it. So could a horse . . . but not while pulling a sled. I grasped the knife. Labelle whinnied again and pulled back.

I heard a sharp bang behind me, followed by movement under my feet. I looked around. The ice had broken. Labelle and I and the sled were now on a pan of ice, a floating slab, and it was starting to tilt under the weight of the sled and its load. If Labelle were still hitched up when the sled slid into the water, I might be able to leap to safety, but she would drown.

Frantically I sawed through the tough leather traces, first the left and then the right. I had them severed just in time. Dropping the knife, I grabbed Labelle by her bridle. We jumped together across the two-foot gap. Behind us, the loose slab tilted backwards. As I watched, the sled slid on its runners across the ice pan and over its edge into the water. Bubbles rose from the sled and its load, now on their way to the bottom of Lake Erie.

I gripped Labelle's bridle. Somehow we made our way, skidding over ridges of broken ice, to the margin of slushy water that rimmed the shore. We splashed our way to solid land, where huge chunks of ice littered the sand. I was soaked in ice water up to my knees. Labelle was shaking. I wrapped my arms around my horse's neck and buried my face in her mane.

"Good girl!" I gasped, almost sobbing. It was too cold to stand there shivering. We needed to find shelter, somewhere warm and dry. We needed to find it without delay.

CHAPTER TWENTY-TWO

ripping Labelle's bridle, I staggered up the beach. The sand was littered with chunks of broken ice. There was a growing numbness in my feet, which felt as though they, too, were chunks of ice. Labelle stamped her hooves.

From the top of the beach I looked back at the white ice pans bobbing on the dark water. Not a trace of the sled or its load remained to be seen. A shock of disbelief hit me. How could something so solid completely disappear, or a weight so heavy be suddenly lifted from my shoulders? I believed in miracles. The Bible was full of them. Now a miracle had saved me—that was how it felt. Nobody could blame me for the ice cracking on Lake Erie. My heart was light, despite the heaviness of my leaden feet and water-logged boots, because now I knew that no blood would be shed through any act of mine.

I pulled out the map Jacob Fox had drawn for me. Not far from here I would find the road that ran all the way along the western shore of Pelee Island to Adam Bruner's place at the southwest tip. Well, I'd follow that road, but only as far as the first house I came to. I'd stop there to ask for help.

I found the road. After that we didn't go far—nothing is far on Pelee Island—before we came to a sturdy-looking log house. Near it stood a log barn. The house had two stone chimneys, one at each end; smoke rising from both. I led Labelle up to the door and knocked.

The man who answered my knock was tall and big-shouldered, his face roughened by wind and sun-glare. Although he looked familiar, I could not think where I had seen him before.

At the sight of me standing there, half-drenched, holding by her bridle a horse in full harness, he cried out, "Good God! What happened?"

"We were crossing from the mainland. The ice broke . . ."

He gave a shout. "Juliana, Henry, everybody! Come here!"

People came running. A middle-aged woman in a homespun dress, a little girl no bigger than my sister Susan, and half a dozen other young people of both sexes. They clustered around the open doorway, staring at Labelle and me. There was something familiar-looking about the entire crowd.

"Come in!" The man opened the door wider."

I shook my head. "Not till I've seen to my horse. Is there room in your barn?" A young fellow stepped forward.

"I'll take care of his horse, Vati."

"No!" I protested." I'll look after her myself!"

"Henry will take care of your horse," the man said in a no-nonsense voice. "You need looking after as much as she does."

Henry picked up a pair of boots from a pile beside the door and pulled them on. He snatched a coat from a hook on the wall and was out the door in a flash. Taking the bridle from my hand, he led Labelle away.

"Now," said the man, "We must get you out of those wet clothes." He held out his hand to grasp mine and pulled me into the house.

The minute I stepped inside into the warmth, I felt my legs collapsing under me. The man caught me as I stumbled. I was half led, half carried to an armchair beside the blazing fire in the fireplace. I lay back in the chair, speechless, while two of the children unlaced my boots and tugged them off. A girl with brown hair stripped off my wet stockings and rubbed my feet. The woman put a glass of brandy to my lips. As I swallowed it, the fiery liquid warmed me all the way down. A dreamy torpor spread through me. The brandy was the last thing I remember clearly. People were asking me questions, but my mind was in such a fog that I don't know what answers I gave.

When I woke up, I found that I had been moved to a settee, where I lay with a pillow under my head and a blanket to cover me. I was alone except for the man who had pulled me in the door. He sat on a stool beside the settee. Lamps were lit. It must be night.

"I see you're awake," he said. "How are you?"

"Groggy."

"You've been asleep for seven hours. The rest of my family have gone to bed. My wife said to offer you bread and butter and a glass of milk when you woke up. Would you like that?"

"Yes," I said, suddenly very hungry.

While he was fetching my food, I sat up and looked around. I saw my boots, placed side by side on the hearth, and my stockings and trousers drying on a rack in front of the fire. Somebody must have taken off my wet trousers without waking me up.

In a few minutes the man was back with the bread and butter and a glass of milk. While I ate, he sat on the stool watching me thoughtfully. When I had finished eating, he said, "Before you completely dropped off to sleep, you were mumbling and muttering. You called me Mr. Fox."

"Did I?"

"How did you know my name?"

I blinked. "Is that your name?"

"I'm George Fox."

Of course! That was why he had looked familiar! Jacob Fox had told me he had three brothers on Pelee Island. This man looked so like Jacob that he might have been his twin. I said, "Jacob Fox of Gosfield Township sent me here. I must have mistaken you for him."

He nodded. "That's easy to do. We're brothers." Then he said, his voice unsteady as if he were afraid to ask, "Who were with you?"

"What do you mean, 'Who were with me?'"

"In your sleigh. I heard you say, 'They're better off at the bottom of the lake.'"

"Oh!" I caught my breath, realizing what he feared. "I was alone. There were no other people." What more should I say? Jacob had told me that his brothers opposed the rebellion. I didn't want to tell this man that I'd been hauling a load of muskets to arm the Patriots. I spoke carefully. "I was pulling a sled, not a sleigh. It was the sled and its load that were better off at the bottom of the lake."

George Fox gave a heavy sigh. "I see. You don't need to explain. My brother Jacob sent you to Pelee Island with a load of something that is better off at the bottom of the lake. I'm not going to ask what it was. I don't want to know how much you're involved, apart from driving the sled. What Jacob is doing amounts to treason. I want to keep my family out of it."

I looked him straight in the eye. "I'm not part of it. I work for a man in Chippawa. He sent me with a load of . . . goods to deliver to Jacob Fox. I didn't know what I was carrying until I reached your brother's home. Then Jacob ordered me to take it to Pelee Island."

"He shouldn't have sent you onto the ice with a heavy load. It wasn't safe."

"He thought it was safe. The day before yesterday, we saw a number of sleighs come across the ice from Pelee Island. They had no problem."

"Those sleighs belonged to William McCormick's family and to some of his tenants. McCormick's people didn't carry any-thing heavy with them—just a few personal possessions. I'm sure the load on your sled weighed much more than what they had in their sleighs." He paused. "Whatever you're carrying, you never can trust the ice. I've lived on Pelee Island for ten years, long enough to know the lake in all seasons. In winter the water is moving under the ice. The current hollows it out from underneath."

That was the end of our discussion. It was late—eleven o'clock, according to the clock on the mantel shelf. "Will you be comfortable sleeping on the settee?" George Fox asked.

"Very comfortable." Then I remembered Labelle. I pushed aside the blanket. "But first, I must see to my horse."

"No need. Just before bedtime, my son Henry went to the barn to check on her. He gave her food and water. Like you, she'll be fine after a good night's rest."

I laid my head back on the pillow and pulled the blanket up to my chin.

In the morning George Fox woke me up at first light. "Your clothes are dry. You can get dressed and come with me to the barn. I need to feed my livestock. You can look after your horse. Juliana will have breakfast ready by the time we return." He gave me a towel and a comb and sent me to the kitchen to make myself tidy. When I'd washed my face and put on my warm, dry trousers and stockings, I pulled on my boots. They were dry but stiff and tight. They felt as though they had shrunk, but that may have been my feet getting too big for my boots, which was something Pa often said about me.

George picked up a bucket of slop that sat by the back door. "This is for the pigs."

I hadn't seen Labelle since the day before, when George's son Henry had led her off to the barn, wet and cold just like me. It turned out I'd had no need to worry. She looked just fine, pricking her ears forward and welcoming me with a toss of her head.

As soon as Labelle and I had both had some food, we'd be ready to cross the ice to the mainland. I was eager to get going. Jacob must be worried about me, because he had expected me back before midnight the previous night. As soon as I'd told Jacob about the loss of the muskets, I could leave on my journey back to Chippawa. With no sled to pull, I could be there in a week.

Those were the thoughts going through my mind when I noticed Labelle's harness hanging on a hook. Henry must have taken it off Labelle and put it there. Looking at the harness, I pictured myself trudging on foot all the way to Chippawa, leading a horse draped with harness. It would not be easy.

George saw the problem. "You need a saddle."

"You're right."

"I have one I can lend you. The harness can stay here in the barn until my next visit to the mainland. Then I'll return it to Jacob and get my saddle back."

"The harness doesn't belong to Jacob. It belongs to . . ." I stopped, warning myself not to name any names. "Anyway, I'll need a saddle all the way back to Chippawa, not just as far as your brother's place."

"Let's take this one step at a time," said George. "Your employer in Chippawa won't expect you to walk two hundred miles leading a horse draped in harness."

"If I borrow a saddle from you, I won't be able to return it. And I don't have money to pay you for it."

"It will all work out. Fortunately, I can afford to give a saddle to a man in need. So if you'll wait here for a minute . . ." He went off to another part of the barn, and when he came back he was carrying a saddle and a saddle pad. Both were well worn but in good shape. He laid them over the edge of a stall. "Here you are. You can saddle her up when you're ready to leave. Now let's do our chores so we can go in for breakfast."

He poured slop from the bucket he had brought from the house into the pigpen trough. There was a big sow and eight piglets. The sow was huge—I'd judge two-hundred-and-fifty pounds. The piglets were big too, maybe forty pounds each. All the hogs stuck their snouts into the trough and snorted as they gobbled up the slop.

"My sow farrowed early," George said. "Those piglets are ready to go to market as feeder pigs." He tended to his horses and cows while I fed and watered Labelle and brushed her mane and tail. He had two good horses that looked fit for harness or saddle, and he had three cows.

We went back to the house. As soon as we opened the door, I smelled bacon frying. I hung up my hat, scarf and coat on a hook by the kitchen door but kept my boots on. The kitchen table was already set for breakfast. The entire family were up and ready to start the day. I'd seen all of them before, but their faces had been a blur. Now we could be properly introduced. There was George's wife Juliana, his son Henry and his daughter Jane, the girl who had taken off my wet stockings and rubbed my feet. Jane was about my age. She looked a lot like Anna, Jacob Fox's book-learned daughter. They were cousins, so that was no surprise. There were other, younger children whose names I forget. All of them called George Fox 'Vati'.

When we were seated at the table, I asked George what Vati meant.

"It's German for Papa. My father was born in Baden County in Germany. He was Vati to his children, and now I'm Vati to mine."

"Your brother Jacob's children call him Vati."

He smiled. "Of course they do. It's our tradition." Then he turned his attention to the food on his plate. He had scarcely lifted his fork when suddenly there was a knock at the door, a knock so loud it made everybody jump. Bang! Bang! Bang!

George raised his head. "Now what?" He pushed his chair back from the table, left the kitchen and opened the front door.

A man's voice bellowed, "I requisition this property in the name of the Republic of Canada. During our occupation of Pelee Island, you will supply lodging and provision for twenty men."

CHAPTER TWENTY-THREE

With a noisy scraping of chair legs, we jumped up from the kitchen table and rushed into the sitting room. The cabin door was wide open. On the threshold stood a short heavy man with bristling straw-coloured whiskers. His hand gripped a flintlock pistol, its muzzle pointed at George Fox's chest. Behind the man crowded a motley crew, some armed with rifles, some with muskets and some with pikes.

George Fox, standing a head taller than the man with the pistol, spoke calmly. "There must be some mistake. I've been promised that the Patriot army will not molest my family or my property. I am no man's enemy. This is not my fight."

The leader glared at George. "This is everybody's fight. If you aren't for us, you're against us." Without turning his head, he barked an order to the men behind him. "Secure the prisoner!"

George shrugged off the first man who grabbed him, pushed away the arm of the next, but made no further resistance. "There's no need to use force," he said quietly, and he allowed the intruders to tie him to the chair, his wrists bound behind the chair back. The Patriots' leader, flourishing his pistol, blustered that swift punishment would follow any show of disrespect to his authority.

The crowd surged from outdoors into the sitting room. They hustled Juliana Fox and the rest of us into the far end of the room. Rounded up like a flock of sheep, we protested feebly. Apart from a few muttered curses and a child's whimpering, the room was quiet.

Then from outdoors came a noise that ripped through the silence. Men shouting. Dogs barking. Pigs squealing. The pigs' horrible squealing was the loudest sound of all. The leader of the invaders laughed. "The boys are getting dinner ready. You can't have roast pork without you slaughter the hog."

I was a farm boy, accustomed to killing food animals. But the sound of that squealing made my blood run cold. Henry looked pale, though I don't suppose he was any more tender-hearted than I when it came to livestock. The noise from outdoors seemed to silence everyone. Men stood still, as if waiting for it to be over. And then it was over. The invaders began to talk and make jokes. The jokes were mostly about food and drink.

These men were soldiers in the Patriot army, but they had no uniforms. Their outer clothes were an assortment of capes, greatcoats, woollen jackets and fringed leather jackets. Their headgear was just as varied: top hats, coonskin hats, workmen's caps and knitted toques.

After taking off their winter wear and dumping it on the floor, the Patriot soldiers made themselves at home. From the kitchen they brought mugs and tumblers, laughing and grinning as they lifted them to their mouths. They drank a toast to the Republic of Canada and then a toast to William Lyon Mackenzie. They toasted various women whom they knew. Someone proposed a toast to Squire William McCormick, thanking him for the barrel of rum they had liberated from his cellar. Their voices rose in a mighty cheer for William McCormick, who had so graciously fled the island, leaving only one servant to guard his home and all its store of food and drink.

Although George Fox remained tied to the chair, the rest of us were free to move about, so long as we stayed in the sitting room. The leader warned that Mr. Fox would pay with his life for any resistance anyone attempted.

Juliana sat by the fire, a blue shawl draped about her shoulders and her younger children clustered around her legs. The smallest, a little girl the same size as my sister Susan, huddled on her mother's lap. Henry sat glowering on a stool in the corner of the room, glaring at the intruders. He looked ready to fight. The threat to kill his father must have stopped him. But what could he have done anyway, one young man against a gang of ruffians? When one of the so-called soldiers spat rudely on the floor, Henry jumped up, his fists clenched; but then he appeared to think better of it. His features twisted with silent rage, he sank back onto the stool.

No one, neither the family nor the invaders, paid any attention to me. I felt invisible. Maybe I could sneak out, somehow get Labelle from the barn, and make a run for it. I peeked through the doorway from the sitting room into the kitchen. There were my coat, hat and scarf on a hook just inside the back door, where I had hung them after returning from the barn. But a couple of Patriots with big knives were standing at the table butchering one of George Fox's forty-pound piglets. The blades of their knives were smeared with blood, and there was a pool of blood on the floor. A fellow with a pike was guarding the door. For the moment, I gave up the idea of escape.

In the sitting room two men were playing cards. They played for money. A jug of rum sat on the table between them. Each player was intent upon the cards he held in his hand. Then one of them looked up. He was good looking, with wavy dark hair, a black moustache, and a sleek smile. I recognized that handsome face. Peter Dash!

So the man whom Laura loved had done what he had said he would do. He had left Anthony's Mills to join the Patriot army, planning to enjoy first the action and then the hundred dollars that William Lyon Mackenzie had promised to recruits. Dash saw me watching him. He looked puzzled for a moment. Then his eyebrows rose. I saw the flash of recognition in his eyes. He sneered at me before returning his attention to the cards he held in his hand.

Dash's opponent was a greasy-looking man wearing stained overalls. On the table in front of him he had a stack of coins.

His brows were drawn together with the mental effort of study-ing his hand of cards. Finally, he threw it down. Dash smiled as he scooped up two coins from the stack in front of his oppo-nent. With his fingers he smoothed his moustache, first one side and then the other. "Shall we have another game? Your luck may change."

"Might as well," the loser muttered. "It can't get any worse."

Dash dealt out the cards. I watched the play—there was nothing else to do while standing there, not free to leave the room. After each game, Dash raked in another two coins. I noticed how he kept filling the other's glass with rum, while the level in his own glass never went down, even though he often raised it to his lips. After a time, Dash's opponent looked as though he could hardly see the cards or sit upright. In the end, he ran out of money. As Dash rose from the table, pock-eting the last of the coins, the loser lowered his head on his hands and sobbed.

"Poor loser!" Dash laughed.

As he was walking away, an onlooker, a muscular heavy-set fellow, grabbed his arm. "You cheated! Give him back his money!"

"The Deuce I will!"

Then the loser's champion threw a punch. Dash reached one arm down to shield his stomach and one arm up to pro-tect his head. But the blow landed in between, on the chest. Dash's breath was expelled with a grunt, and he fell over back-wards to the floor.

That was the signal for a brawl to begin. The Patriot soldiers had been drinking rum for the past four hours. All discipline abandoned, they jumped into the fray. Their leader screamed for order. No one listened. I took advantage of the confusion and sneaked into the empty kitchen. The drying blood of the slaughtered pigs felt sticky under my boots. I snatched up my coat, hat and scarf from the hook, and slipped out the back door.

CHAPTER TWENTY-FOUR

I ducked around the corner of the cabin, carrying my outer clothes that I had pulled from the hook beside the door. I could still hear the ruckus going on inside—shouts and thuds and a child's frightened cry. There were no windows on this side of the cabin. No one indoors could see me while I was I putting on my coat, scarf and hat. I was fairly safe as long as I stayed here. But I had to get to the barn, and that meant cross- ing the barnyard, an open space two hundred feet wide, where I could be seen by anyone looking out the kitchen window.

I stuck out my head and peered around the corner of the cabin. The barnyard was a shambles, the snow littered with heaps of guts—offal from the slaughter of George Fox's hogs— and soaked with blood. Not dark like dried blood. The pigs' blood had frozen before it had time to dry.

Looking across the barnyard, I saw two men and a sleigh in front of the barn door. Hitched to the sleigh was a fran- tic horse. He was a black gelding, about sixteen hands, with powerful shoulders and hindquarters. Panicked by the sight and smell of blood, he was tossing his head and pawing the ground. His ears were flat back, his eyes wide and wild look- ing. He struck out with his back feet, his hooves crashing into the front of the sleigh.

One man was sitting in the sleigh driver's seat, wedged between two huge half-carcasses, each as big as he was. So these looters had butchered the mother sow, cleaving her from snout to tail. The other man stood at the horse's head, gripping the bridle with both hands. The man on the sleigh got down to help his comrade steady the horse. Now there were two of them at the horse's head, pulling him by the bridle to turn him around so that he would no longer be able to see the blood on the snow. It isn't easy to turn around a kicking horse that's hitched up to a loaded sleigh. They were determined. I reckoned that sooner or later they would succeed. But by then more looters may have arrived. Labelle was in the barn—at least I hoped and prayed she was still in the barn. What a prize that fine Canadian horse would be for some American rascal to take back to Sandusky! So I was silently cheering on the two men as they struggled to control their horse, which they finally succeeded in doing, leading him in a big wide arc until they had him facing the opposite direction.

Now they both climbed into the sleigh, the driver again wedged between the two halves of George's Fox's sow, and the other man sharing the passengers' seat with the carcasses of two large piglets. On that sleigh were a good three hundred pounds of pork on their way to somebody's kitchen in Sandusky.

With a jangle of bells, the sleigh headed off down the lane. Now the coast was clear. My fingers crossed that Labelle would still be in the barn, I raced across the barnyard. When I opened the barn door and saw her, it seemed too good to be true. But there she was, along with George Fox's two horses and three cows. The barn floor was smeared with trampled pig manure, which was no surprise, considering the state the hogs must have been in as men dragged them squealing from the barn. The cows were mooing mournfully, and I could see why. Their udders were swollen full. Somebody should have milked them hours ago. I pitied the poor beasts.

All three horses snorted when they saw me. They pointed their ears right at me. I knew what this meant. They wanted food. They wanted water. But I had no time to spare. At any moment, more looters might arrive. I didn't want any Patriot soldiers finding me here.

The used saddle that George Fox had offered me was still resting on the edge of the stall where he had put it. I saddled Labelle, led her from the barn and closed the door behind me.

Before leaving, I took a last look at the house. From this distance I could hear nothing. Maybe the brawl had ended. Whether or not it was over, there was no way I could help George Fox and his family. It was wrong to leave without thanking them for giving shelter to me and my horse, and I felt bad about that. As for Peter Dash, by now the man who had caught him cheating at cards may have beaten him senseless. If so, he had it coming. Dash's fate was not my concern.

When I was mounted, I put Labelle into a canter as fast as I could. The ride was good for both of us. It was a clear day, as bright and cold as an icicle. I was eager to return to the mainland. Jacob Fox must be worried about me—and about the muskets. But before we started across the ice, Labelle needed food and water. I could think of only one person likely to provide these: Adam Bruner. He was expecting forty muskets; I had to tell him what had happened to those guns. Knowing I'd been sent by Jacob Fox, Bruner would take pity on me and on my horse. I felt sure he'd give both of us something to eat before we faced the twenty-mile trek to the mainland. It was early in the afternoon. I had time to report to Adam Bruner, rest Labelle for an hour, and still be back at Jacob Fox's farm by midnight.

CHAPTER TWENTY-FIVE

We had travelled at a fine canter for half a mile when suddenly the road ahead was blocked by a flock of bleating sheep. Baa! Baa! Baa! There were about fifty sheep, as round as barrels in their heavy fleece. Two men were with them, one on either side of the road. But it wasn't the men who were in charge of the sheep. Two dogs were doing the real work of moving the flock.

Labelle and I came to a stop. Labelle snorted. When the dogs saw that I wanted to pass, they exchanged a glance and, moving as a team, expertly manoeuvered the flock off the road. They were ordinary farm dogs, their shaggy coats a mixture of black, brown and white. They looked like the dog we had on our farm back home. Our dog's name was Tray. Seeing these dogs work the flock made me feel homesick, but only for a moment.

I was tempted to ask the men what they thought they were doing, moving sheep at this time of year, when the ewes were nearly ready to drop their spring lambs. Snow covered all the fields, so it wasn't as though they were taking the flock to better pasture. But I knew better than to ask such a question, because it was perfectly clear that those sheep were on their way to Sandusky, woolly prisoners of war.

As I rode by, the men gave me a wave and a big smile. One called out, "That's a mighty fine horse you've got yourself!" Then the truth hit me: those rascals thought I'd stolen my horse from somebody's barn here on Pelee Island, just as they had stolen the sheep. Well, I wasn't about to change their minds. My best protection was to pose as a looter from Ohio, just like them. So I gave a cheery wave as I rode by.

I had slowed Labelle to a walk while passing the sheep. When the flock was behind us, I put her back into a canter. It didn't last long before we came upon another obstacle. Two drovers on horseback were moving a herd of cattle toward the south end of the island. More spoils of war. These were milk cows, their udders swaying. I rode around the herd, giving a nod to the drovers as I went by. They looked like farmers, even though armed with rifles. Patriot soldiers taking Pelee Island livestock back to Ohio.

The further I went, the more crowded the road became. We passed sleds and sleighs laden with bulging grain sacks, cow hides, apple barrels, sides and quarters of beef and pork and skinned lamb carcasses. I saw a pile of dead chickens sharing a sled with a whetstone and a spinning wheel. Another sled was heaped with shiny glass objects that flashed and sparkled and gleamed in the sunshine. Some flared with colours like a rainbow. What was this? Then it came to me. I was looking at the lamps, lenses and mirrors from the lantern of the Pelee Island lighthouse. Was there nothing that these bandits would not steal? The Patriot invasion of Canada looked more like a looting expedition than a military action. Why did the Patriots need forty muskets? Why did they need any? Whom were they going to fight? There were no Canadian or British troops stationed on Pelee Island. The people had no defence.

Jacob Fox had told me to watch for Adam Bruner's name on a board nailed to a fence post. At last I saw it! The nine-mile ride from the north end of Pelee Island had taken twice as long as I had expected. I rode up Bruner's lane and dismounted at the front door. At my knock, the door was opened by a small, shriveled elderly man. His clothes hung loosely upon him, as if he had shrunk but they had not. He was completely bald. His face was wrinkled like a dried apple, and his eyes were small and dark.

"What do you want?" he asked before I had time to introduce myself.

"I . . . I've come from the mainland. Jacob Fox sent me with a load of muskets." His head darted forward as he peered beyond me. "Where are they, then?"

"Er . . . at the bottom of the lake. The ice broke."

"Did you come here to tell me that?" There was something snakelike about the way he darted his head forward and fixed me with his small, dark eyes.

"I felt I should report to you before going back to the mainland."

"I suppose you want a place to stay tonight. You lose the muskets and then expect me to give you room and board?"

"I don't need lodging. I'm going back to Jacob Fox's place as soon as I've rested my horse. She needs food and water." I decided not to mention that I could use some food and water, too.

"It's four o'clock in the afternoon. Only a fool would start across the lake this late in the day."

I didn't know what time it was, although the shadows on the snow should have told me.

But Adam Bruner looked so mean that I'd be jiggered if I'd ask *him* for shelter. On the other hand, I didn't want Labelle and me to perish out on the ice.

Bruner saved me from the need to ask for lodging. After giving me a grunt of disdain and a look of contempt, he turned his head and shouted to someone inside the house, "Betty, we have a guest. Put on the kettle."

In a moment Betty appeared. She was a fluttery-looking, little woman wearing a dark dress and a white mob cap that had a lace frill all around the bottom. Bruner said to her, "This boy lost the load of muskets Jacob Fox was sending over."

Before I could protest that I did not "lose" them, Betty said in a quavering voice, "That's the best news I've heard in days."

Bruner scowled at her. "Get back to the kitchen and make tea." She fluttered away. Under his breath he muttered, "Tender-hearted fool!" Then he darted his head at me. "I'll take you to the barn to stable your horse."

CHAPTER TWENTY-SIX

In Adam Bruner's barn were two horses, one cow, and half a dozen pigs. Bruner pointed to an empty stall. "Put your mare in that one. The pump's in the yard. The hay's in the loft. Take what you need. When you're done, I'll see you inside."

After he left, I climbed the ladder to the loft. It was a sweet-smelling space, with a small window that looked out over Pelee Island's southern tip, a long tapering point of land—a funnel through which Pelee Islanders' goods were pouring to new homes in Ohio. As I stood watching, a loaded sled pulled by a pair of horses reached the very tip, hesitated, then bumped from the shore onto the ice. Further south in the distance were more sleds and sleighs, those furthest away no larger than ants as they crept along the ice road to Sandusky.

Disgusted, I stopped watching. After pitching down a few flakes of hay for Labelle, I joined her below. After I'd fed her, I gave her a good rubdown and checked her feet. My horse's company was more pleasant than Bruner's, so I took my time. When I returned to the house, Betty was sitting on the edge of a wooden chair, looking ready to spring up at her husband's command. Bruner was lounging in an easy chair by the fire. I sat down at the table, where Betty had placed a plate of cookies, which were very good. The tea was already cold. That was my fault, because I'd spent so long in the barn.

I thanked her for the tea and cookies. While I ate, Bruner explained his wife's comment about the muskets. "Betty doesn't like the idea of bloodshed. Maybe this time she's right. The smart move for this Patriot army is go right back to Sandusky before anybody gets hurt."

I replied, "From the number of sleds and sleighs heading south, I'd say that's already happening."

He nodded. "Two days ago we had a thousand men on Pelee Island. Half of them came to loot. No doubt about that. But the other half had a purpose that's nobler than greed. They came to occupy Pelee Island as a first step to freeing Canada from British rule. The problem is, there's hardly one real soldier in the lot. Next time we try to liberate Canada, we'd better have a trained army to do it. This rebellion is turning into a farce."

"I just hope it ends without anybody being hurt," Betty said plaintively. Then she hopped up from her chair. "I'll make fresh tea."

While she was busy in the kitchen, Bruner kept on talking. "The Patriot army has some good leaders. I'm impressed by Major Lester Hoadley and Captain Henry Van Rensselaer. Van Rensselaer sets up drills and military exercises to train the recruits. Unfortunately, there's not enough time for that! Within two days, they'll be facing a real army."

"A real army? What do you mean?"

"The invasion began five days ago. William McCormick saw it coming. By now, he's had plenty of time to send word to Colonel Maitland at Fort Malden. It won't take Maitland more than three days to mount an army. A real army! Some of Maitland's British Regulars are veterans of the Battle of Waterloo. As soon as their officers, shout 'Fix bayonets! Charge!' our so-called soldiers will scatter like a flock of wild turkeys." Bruner lifted his head and glared at me, as if the unpreparedness of the Patriot army were somehow my fault.

Betty's voice rang out. "Here's a fresh pot of tea." She appeared from the kitchen carrying the teapot on a tray. But before she could reach the table with it, a deafening burst of gunfire shook the house. It was like a clap of thunder right overhead. The tray fell from Betty's hands.

I jumped up and rushed to the window. Through clouds of smoke I saw a crowd of men milling about in the field beyond the house

"What's going on?"

"Battle practice," said Bruner. "It's a military exercise. I let them use my field." He had not moved from his comfortable chair.

When the smoke cleared, I saw half a dozen bodies lying motionless on the trampled snow. But there was no blood. Some men were snatching up guns from the bodies. Another man held high a pole from which waved a most unusual flag. It was divided into two halves, upper and lower. The upper half was blue, with two big white stars side by side. The lower half was white, with the word LIBERTY spelled out in red letters.

"What's that flag?" I asked.

He rose from his chair and came to the window. "It's the flag of the Republic of Canada. The stars stand for Upper Canada and Lower Canada, the two States of the new Republic."

Why stars? I wondered. *An American must have designed that flag.*

As I watched, the bodies lying on the snow came to life and rose to their feet. An officer in a greatcoat waved his sword and shouted commands. A second officer pointed with his sword, directing the men to form up in two lines.

"That's Captain Van Rensselaer in the greatcoat," said Bruner. "The other officer is Major Hoadley. There aren't enough guns for everyone, so the officers have the men form up in two lines. The men in the front line have rifles or muskets—whatever's available. The second line is unarmed. When the battle begins and both sides have fired a volley, the men in the second line must rush forward to pick up the weapons of their fallen comrades." Bruner darted an accusing look at me. "That's what you have to do when the muskets you need are lying at the bottom of Lake Erie."

I didn't answer. After watching a minute longer, I turned away. Betty was on her knees picking up shards of the broken teapot. She looked up mournfully. "I'll have to make our tea in a saucepan." Her voice was shaky. I knelt beside her to pick up small pieces she missed. The tea had splashed everywhere, soaking the rag rug on the floor.

A few minutes later there was another explosion of gunfire. Again the house shook. "This is the last time they'll practice today," said Bruner. "It's getting dark."

I joined Bruner and his wife for supper. It was a good meal. We had mashed potatoes, turnips and ham, followed by a rice pudding full of raisins and sprinkled with cinnamon. Bruner complained that there was too much salt in the potatoes and not enough sugar in the pudding. When we finished eating, Betty offered to make me up a bed for the night.

"No, thank you," I said to her. "That's very kind, but if you can spare me an old blanket, I'd like to sleep in the loft. With so many soldiers running amok, I'm afraid someone might break into the barn. If I'm sleeping in the loft, I can protect my horse."

"Where you sleep is up to you," said Bruner. "But the Patriots know better than to harm any property of mine."

Betty brought me a patchwork quilt. I said goodnight and went out to the barn with the quilt over my arm. The loft was not too cold, because the rising body heat from the livestock below took the edge off the chill in the air. I rolled up in the thick quilt. The sweet-smelling hay made a soft bed. As I lay with my face turned toward the window, I could see millions of stars. They made me think how big the world was, and how far away was my home.

Pa had warned me to avoid border towns where Patriots had their Hunters' Lodges. But I'd walked straight into their midst the very first day I left home. I should have heeded Pa's warning. As soon as I returned to Chippawa, I'd tell Mr. Kemp I needed to find employment elsewhere. I'd take Pa's advice and look for work in those peaceful settlements where I'd stayed along the Talbot Road. I was big and strong. I'd work hard. As soon as I'd earned enough money, I'd buy a horse to replace old Prince. More than anything else in the world, I wanted to be back home.

CHAPTER TWENTY-SEVEN

The blare of a bugle jolted me awake in the morning. Partly wrapped in the quilt and partly dragging it behind me, I stumbled to the loft window. What I saw made my heart drop down into my boots. Stretched out on the ice was a long, long line of redcoats, about one hundred men.

They stood evenly spaced about two yards apart, looking like fence posts. So Colonel Maitland's troops had arrived from Fort Malden to drive out the Patriot invaders. Adam Bruner had told me yesterday that it wouldn't take more than two days for Colonel Maitland and his army to arrive. Here they were! Maitland sure didn't waste any time.

The redcoats were lined up facing the shore, which meant that they were facing me. The barrels of their muskets rested on their shoulders. As I watched, an officer in a grey overcoat raised his sword. At that signal the soldiers swung their muskets forward. They looked ready for battle. But where was the enemy?

Then I saw the enemy, streaming in a solid column from the shore onto the ice, led by a standard-bearer carrying that peculiar flag with its two white stars and the word LIBERTY in red letters. I recognized the two officers, Captain Van Rensselaer and Major Hoadley, who had been drilling the Patriot soldiers in Bruner's field. As the men spread out over the ice, they formed up in two lines, just they had done in battle practice. The men in the front line were armed, some with rifles and some with muskets. The men in the line behind them had no weapons.

Now the enemy forces faced each other, their battle lines just about equal in length The Patriots, in two ranks, had more men; but the redcoats had more guns.

I wasn't afraid. It didn't occur to me that I should be afraid. In an odd way, I felt above the scene that was about to unfold. I was obviously above it physically, the ice on the lake being some thirty feet below my vantage point. But the feeling wasn't just because I was watching from above. It was as if I had been set there for a purpose. Whatever the reason, no mere accident had placed me by this window.

The Patriots fired first. Fire spurted from the barrels of their guns. At once the redcoats returned their fire. The blast of noise rattled the window of the loft and shook the rafters. From below me in the barn came the terrified whinnying of the horses, the bellowing of Bruner's cow and the squealing of his pigs. Out on the ice, the black powder threw up a cloud of smoke.

Through the smoke I saw bodies lying on the ice and Patriot soldiers snatching up the guns of their fallen comrades the way they'd been drilled to do. But this time the motionless bodies did not come to life again.

There was another volley of rapid fire from both sides, the noise deafening and then subsiding. As before, the Patriot soldiers who had no guns scrambled to pick up the firearms of the wounded and the dead. Then the cavalry arrived, twenty mounted men galloping from around the southeast end of the island, their leader brandishing his sword. The horsemen halted and fired.

Now the Patriot soldiers were in a bad spot, with the cavalry attacking their flank and the line of redcoats facing them. At first, they kept their heads. They fired. They reloaded. They fired again. For every man that fell, another came forward to pick up his weapon. I didn't think about which side was going to win. I just watched.

Then the British officer gave the command. "Fix bayonets! Charge!" I caught my breath at the sight of those gleaming bayonet blades a foot and a half long. The infantry charged, their bright steel flashing in the sunshine. The Patriot battle line wavered. Then the men broke and ran. They scattered in all directions like wild turkeys, just as Adam Bruner had said they would.

Captain Van Rensselaer tried to rally his troops. He was flourishing his sword when suddenly he seemed to leap high in the air, as if he had been lifted off his feet by the force of the bullet that struck him. He dropped to the ice and lay motionless in a pool of blood. I looked for the other Patriot officer, Major Hoadley, but did not see him for the smoke.

Some of the fleeing Patriot soldiers were running back to the island, where I supposed they would try to hide in the woods, but most were heading south over the ice. Redcoats pursued them, lunging after the fleeing enemy with their bayonets. The cavalry bore down on them. The ice was stained red with blood. The flag of the Republic of Canada lay trampled underfoot.

I watched a redcoat gain on a fleeing man. When the point of the bayonet barely touched his back, it was enough to make him stumble. He was on his knees when the bayonet plunged hard into his back. The man crumpled to the ice. There was no blood until the redcoat yanked the bayonet out of the body, putting one foot on the small of the man's back as he pulled. Then blood poured as fast as water when an ice jam on a creek breaks in spring.

The redcoat straightened up and looked about, like a hunter searching for new prey. He spotted another fleeing man and started after him, ready to do it again. Smeared with blood, the blade of his bayonet did not shine as brightly as it had before. I looked away, not wanting to see more.

Then it was finished. The shooting stopped and the smoke cleared. The entire battle had not lasted longer than an hour. Several redcoats, soldiers who had not joined in pursuit of the fleeing Patriots, were tending to the wounded, both their own and the enemy casualties. Sleighs that had been parked further out on the ice came to the battle site to carry off the wounded and the dead. Captured Patriot soldiers were marched away under guard.

For a long time I sat there by the window. I felt very thirsty and wished I had a tumbler of fresh water to drink. But I didn't seem to have the power to do anything about my thirst. I had seen a battle, and I realized even then that I did not ever want to see another.

I wondered how Bruner and his wife were faring. They too must have witnessed the battle, although their view could not have been as wide and clear as mine. But no. Betty would not have seen it. She would have covered her eyes and her ears or fled into a different room. I'd have to wait until the coast was clear to find out how they were. For now, I'd better stay up here in the barn loft, out of sight. If the redcoats saw me, they'd mistake me for a Patriot soldier and carry me off to Fort Malden as a prisoner of war. A new thought occurred to me. What about Adam Bruner? Did anyone in Maitland's army know that he was helping the enemy? I half expected to see the old man dragged out of his house and marched away with the prisoners of war.

Below me in the barn, the horses had stopped whinnying. The cow's bellowing and the hogs' squealing had ceased. *I'd better go down and look after Labelle*, I thought. I still had the quilt pulled around me. I unwrapped myself the rest of the way, put on my coat, and was just about to descend from the loft when I paused to take a final look out the window.

There was Colonel Maitland's army—sleds, sleighs, redcoats and prisoners—already half a mile away, heading northeast on their march back to the mainland, returning to Fort Malden, their mission complete.

Then something closer caught my eye, a man carrying a box under his arm, walking fast across Bruner's field, head-ing for the shore. The box was the same size as a family Bible. The man's elbow was stuck out to fit it under his arm, and his hand gripped its lower front corner. He was tall and slender. I couldn't see his face because his back was to me. When he reached the shore, he stopped and looked over his shoulder as if checking to see whether he was being followed. When he turned, I saw his face. Clean shaven. Dark moustache. It was the handsome face of Peter Dash. Apparently reassured that no one was following him, he stepped from the shore onto the ice and started walking again. He was walking so fast he looked ready to break into a run.

The last time I had seen Dash was in the sitting room of George Fox's house, when he was being pummelled by the man who caught him cheating at cards. That was yesterday. Where had he been since then? He could not have been in the battle—not while carrying that box. What was in the box? It wasn't clear to me where he was going, just that he was leaving Pelee Island as quickly as he could. Something told me that I must not let him get away.

CHAPTER TWENTY-EIGHT

A s soon as I had my hat on my head and my scarf around my neck, I clambered down the ladder from the loft. Labelle whinnied as I ran by. "I'll be back!" I shouted. Thump, thump, thump went my heart against my ribs as I tore out of the barn and raced to the shore and out onto the ice.

Although the smoke of battle had cleared, the smell of gunpowder lingered in the air.

Peter Dash was still in plain sight. Now it was clear where he was going—northwest to the Canadian mainland. Coming after him as fast as I could, I'd catch up with him soon. He was taller and bigger than I. In a fight, he would have the advantage. I didn't worry about that. As soon as I was close enough for him to hear me, I hollered, "Stop!"

He turned his head and saw me. If it hadn't been for my coonskin hat and long red scarf, he might not have recognized me. I'd been wearing both when he met me the first time, which was at the sawmill in Anthony's Mills. And he had definitely recognized me during the card game at George's Fox's home. So he knew who I was. Seeing me coming after him, he probably didn't know what to do. He simply started running. Maybe he thought he could outrun me, even carrying the box.

There were breaks in the ice, deep cracks, and places where the slabs tilted up and over one another. Dash ran a zigzag course, almost losing his balance several times. Yet still he kept the box under his arm. I had almost reached him, when suddenly the ice cracked. A gap opened just ahead. Dash tried to

stop. Sliding, skidding, he was almost at the brink of the yawn-
ing gap when he lost his balance. Flinging both arms into the
air in a desperate, instinctive attempt not to fall, he dropped
the box. I saw it hit the ice and burst open, spilling its contents. At the same time, Dash slid into the water, and I heard
him scream.

I stopped cold. His gloved hands clawed desperately at the
edge. The ice was a foot thick, but there was nothing to grip.

"Help me!" he gasped.

It took a moment for my mind to tell my body what to do.
I dropped to my hands and knees to distribute my weight
while I crawled toward him. One yard from the edge, I stopped.
Although I could have reached out and grasped his hand, we
would both have ended up in the water if I did that. We stared
into each other's eyes. In his eyes I saw terror and a mute appeal,
but no hope. The only sounds were his panting breath and the
scraping of his gloves against the ice.

If I'd had a plank, I could have pushed it out over the ice
so that he could grab it and pull himself up upon it. If I'd had
a rope, I could have thrown it to him. I had neither. What did
I have? Just my scarf, the six-foot-long red muffler that my
mother had knitted for me. Hastily I unwound it from around
my neck. Dash's frantic eyes were upon me as I rolled it up.
Rising onto my knees, I gripped one end and hurled the balled-
up scarf to him, using the same motion that I'd use to cast a
line with a fishing rod. The free end of my scarf landed at the
very edge of the ice.

"Grab hold!" I yelled. "I'll pull you out."

He grabbed his end, and I held tight to mine. I pulled with all
my might, still on my knees, backing away from the edge. It felt
as if I were hauling in a big fish, like a muskie. That scarf must
have stretched an extra yard by the time I had Dash out of the
water and lying face down on the ice, still gripping his end of
my scarf. Then I stood up. As soon as I felt steady on my feet,
I dragged him on his belly back to solid ice. As I clasped him

under both arms, he let go of my scarf. I pulled him upright, and tried to plant him on his feet. He could not stand alone. I grasped his upper arm, gripping it firmly.

"We're going back to Pelee Island," I told him.

He said not a word. He did not look at me. His eyes were on the box and what it had held. I followed his gaze. Jewellery. Bracelets and necklaces and brooches glittering and gleaming in the sunshine. He stared for a moment at the treasure that lay scattered upon the ice, and then he looked away.

Water dripped from the drooping corners of his black moustache. His face was dead white, apart from a purplish bruise under one half-closed eye. The pummelling he took yesterday must have caused that bruise. He began to tremble, his whole body shaking violently. "Lean on me," I said. "You must keep moving." I tugged his arm across my shoulders. "Let's go!"

The only place I could think to take him was Adam Bruner's house. Bruner might not want to help him, but Betty would take him in. "Tender-hearted fool" her husband had called her. Some folks might say the same about me. I could have let Dash drown. I could abandon him right now, let him collapse on the ice and freeze while I gathered up the jewellery to keep for myself. Doing that might have made things easier, not just for me but also for love-struck Laura. *She wouldn't thank me*, I thought, *but her life would be easier if Dash ceased to exist.*

He was half a head taller than me, maybe twenty pounds heavier, and I was bearing most of his weight. It was the longest half mile I ever walked. Simply to put one foot ahead of the other was all I could do. But I didn't forget the sight of that jewellery left lying on the ice. Dash had stolen it, of course. Whose jewellery was it? It didn't take me long to figure that out. Only one family on Pelee Island was rich enough. The McCormicks.

I pieced together what might have happened after I sneaked away from George Fox's home. Dash knew that the McCormicks had fled from the island. They must have been in a terrible panic, to forget to take that jewellery with them. Everyone in

George Fox's sitting room had heard the toast to William McCormick. The invaders had cheered him for leaving his house on Pelee Island with just one servant to guard it. What an amazing opportunity! There's no telling what a thief might find to steal! And so, instead of risking his life in battle, Dash had sneaked away on his own to break into their house. Those bracelets, necklaces and brooches must be worth a good deal more than the hundred dollars William Lyon Mackenzie offered to recruits.

My mind was busy while I tottered across the ice, half carrying Peter Dash. By the time we reached Bruner's house, I had a plan. I would not breathe a word about that jewellery to Adam Bruner or Betty. As soon as I had left Dash there, I was going back to gather it up. Not for myself—not for a moment did I think of that. *Honesty is its own reward.* That's another thing Ma used to say. I know it's true. But I was hoping that when I returned the jewellery, Mr. McCormick would do more to show his gratitude than just thank me and shake my hand.

CHAPTER TWENTY-NINE

It was hot work, lugging Peter Dash across the ice. I didn't feel the cold, even though I wasn't wearing my scarf or my hat. My scarf was lying where I had left it. I didn't know what had become of my hat. It must have been knocked from my head somewhere along the way. By the time I reached Bruner's house, I was ready to collapse. When I knocked, Betty opened the door.

"Oh!" she gasped when she saw us, then she stood back to let us stagger inside, Dash draped over my shoulder.

"He was running away. He fell through the ice," I paused to catch my breath. "I pulled him out of the water."

"He's lucky you were there."

There was a wooden bench by the door, handy for a person to sit while putting on his boots. Betty pulled Dash's free arm across her narrow shoulders, and together we helped him to the bench. Adam Bruner got up from his easy chair by the fire and jutted his leathery face in the direction of the dripping man.

"Who's this? Why did you bring him here?"

His second question was the only one I answered. "Your house was the closest place."

"You bring nothing but trouble." he turned his glare on me.

"Oh, dear! That poor man!" Betty bustled about. "We must get him out of those wet clothes. I'll fetch a blanket."

Muttering furiously, Bruner watched while I stripped off Dash's clothes and wrapped him in the woollen blanket that Betty brought. He grumpily stepped out of the way to allow us to settle Dash in the easy chair by the fire, where he lay back against the pillows. His teeth chattered, his face was ghastly white, and his black moustaches drooped damply past the corners of his mouth. Bruner stood by and glowered.

"I'll make tea," said Betty, "and add a dash of brandy." Then she looked at me. "You need some, too. And you must dry your coat. It's wet from carrying that man."

I took off my coat, which certainly had soaked up a lot of water. Soon the tea was ready. Dash was trembling so violently that Betty had to hold the cup to his mouth. After slobbering a few drops down his chin, Dash downed it eagerly. Not being accustomed to strong liquor, I was slower to drink mine.

Between sips, I asked Bruner and Betty. "Did you see the battle?"

"We drew the curtains," said Betty. "Adam watched through the crack. I couldn't bear to look."

"It was a disgrace!" Bruner growled. "But no worse than I expected."

"When it was over," said Betty, "some soldiers from Colonel Maitland's army came to check that we didn't have any fugitives hiding here. We didn't mention you up in the barn loft."

"I'm not a fugitive!" I protested.

"When you didn't show up after the battle, that's what we thought," said Bruner. "Then I checked the barn and saw your horse still there. So I knew we hadn't got rid of you."

"We're so glad to see you safe and sound," said Betty.

"Speak for yourself, woman!" Bruner snapped.

As we talked, I finished my tea and brandy. Its warmth spread through my body, but my mind stayed clear. I knew exactly what I had to do next. I set my empty cup on the table. "Thank you for your hospitality and for giving shelter to this man. I'm going to the barn to saddle my horse. I'll fetch the quilt you were so kind to lend me. Then I'll be on my way."

"Adam can get the quilt next time he goes out to the barn," said Betty. "But you shouldn't be in a hurry to leave. Your coat is still wet. Stay till it's dry."

Steam was rising from my coat, and it smelled like a wet dog. I put it on anyway. "If I leave now, I can reach the mainland before dark. I've left my hat and scarf out on the ice. I'll pick them up on my way."

At the word scarf, Dash raised his head. Our eyes met. He knew that if I hadn't already noticed the jewellery scattered on the ice, I'd be sure to see it when I went back for the scarf. Whatever I did with that treasure, it was lost to him, and he dare not say a word. Frustration, fury and despair were printed on every line of his face.

When I entered the barn, Labelle gave a snort. I read the reproach in her eyes. *What took you so long?* I stroked her neck and rubbed her soft nose. "Sorry. There was a problem, but we can leave now." It looked as though Bruner had fed and watered her along with his livestock. I saddled her up. She pranced as I led her from the barn, so I knew she forgave me. When I was up in the saddle, she tossed her head, eager to be off.

As soon as we were past the rubble of broken ice along the shore, I put her into a canter.

We stopped partway to pick up my hat, where it had fallen off. Ahead of me I saw the gap in the ice and the strip of dark water. There was my scarf lying stretched out and the jewellery box wide open, its velvet lining as red as my scarf. Most of the jewellery had spilled from the box and lay scattered where it had fallen. Gold, silver and precious stones glittered and gleamed in the sunshine. I could hardly believe they were real, not a dream. I halted Labelle a safe distance from the break in the ice. When I had dismounted, I told her, "Wait here!"

The jewellery and the open box lay close to the edge of the ice. I approached cautiously. It was a pity I couldn't just put the jewels back in the box, but there was no way I could carry it without its being seen. It was fashioned of polished wood, with brass corners. There were eight little slots for rings. Seven rings were still in the slots. One slot was empty. I pulled the rings from their slots and tried to put them on my fingers because that was the easiest and safest way to carry them. But

my knuckles were too big. Among the necklaces was a locket
on a silver chain. I undid its clasp and slid all seven rings onto
the chain and fastened it around my neck. A string of pearls,
a rope of jet beads and a little gold cross on a gold chain also
went around my neck. There were five bracelets, all of them
set with different coloured gemstones. I fastened the bracelets
around my wrists. I stuffed my pockets with brooches. Ma used
to tell me that I was worth my weight in gold; at that moment
it was certainly true.

I considered throwing the jewellery box into the water. But
it was too beautiful to destroy. It would have floated, anyway.
So I left it lying there for someone to discover, wondering what
the finder would think and what he would do about it.

The end of my scarf that Dash had clutched was frozen stiff.
Rather than wrap my scarf around my neck, I tied it around
my waist. When I saw my mother again, I'd tell her how the
scarf she'd knitted for me had saved a man's life.

After waiting patiently for me, Labelle was eager to be
underway. Twenty miles due north lay Jacob's Fox's farm near
Albertville. But my first destination was not Albertville; it was
Colchester, further west along the Lake Erie shore. That was
where the McCormicks were going when they fled from Pelee
Island. Jacob had told me that they owned another home there.
I kept my eyes open for cracks in the ice. There were a few
tricky spots; but with no sled to pull, we made good progress.
This was the course that the McCormicks had followed with
loaded sleighs, and they had come to no harm.

As I rode, I thought about Peter Dash back on Pelee Island,
warming up beside Adam Bruner's fire. He would not stay there
long. Bruner would push him out the door as soon as Betty
had dried his clothes. Then where would Dash go? There was
no chance he'd ever collect the hundred dollars that William
Lyon Mackenzie had promised to recruits. The stolen jewellery
was gone. He couldn't make much of a living from cheating
at cards. So what would Dash do to repair his fortunes? The

answer was obvious: he would marry Laura, the love-struck rich girl who wanted to run away with him. It was up to me to stop this from happening. I had to warn Laura, tell her what her sweetheart was really like. If she wouldn't listen, I'd tell her grandparents. Laura would hate me for that. But so what? On my way back to Chippawa, I must stop in Fort Erie at the home of Mr. and Mrs. Goodwin. There was little time to lose.

But first of all, before anything else, I had to return the jewellery to Mr. McCormick and his family. Colchester was sure to have a tavern where I could ask directions to their home. The McCormicks wouldn't know about the battle on the ice because there had not been enough time for a message from Colonel Maitland to reach them. But I had seen it, and I could tell them about it. That was where my story must begin.

It was a cold day. As my soggy coat lost the warmth it had absorbed from the Bruners' fire, the chill crept into my bones. The north wind stabbed like a knife. I was half frozen by the time I saw a church steeple above the trees ahead. *That must be Colchester. Thank God!* I would be there soon.

CHAPTER THIRTY

The first stars were twinkling in the sky by the time I had Labelle's reins looped over the hitching post in front of William McCormick's house. I knocked at the front door, knowing exactly what I planned to say. First I would tell the McCormicks about the battle, and then I would give them the jewellery. I could imagine their excitement. I had not long to wait before the door was opened by a gentleman of middle age. Clean-shaven and slightly plump, he had the look of a man of action despite his greying hair and well-fed look.

"Sir," I began, "have I the honour of speaking with Mr. William McCormick?"

He looked at me gravely. "I am William McCormick." He opened the door wider and motioned me to enter. I stepped gladly into the warmth of his front hall and pulled off my hat. He closed the door.

"What is it?" he asked. "What business brings you here?"

"Sir, I've just come from Pelee Island. There's been a battle. Colonel Maitland's army has driven the invaders from the island." I expected him to cheer. Instead, a shadow passed over his face.

"A battle? Already? What about my sons—John, William, David?" His voice quavered. "They were with Maitland."

"Your sons? I . . . I don't know."

"But you must know whether my sons are wounded or dead!" For the first time, he took a good look at me, with my coon-skin hat in my hand and the long scarf knotted around my middle. He steadied his voice. "What's this all about? When did this battle take place? John Maitland wouldn't send a boy like you to make a report. He'd send a soldier. Where is Colonel Maitland now?"

"The battle was fought this morning. By now Colonel Maitland is back at Fort Malden with his army." I hesitated. "But, Sir, I don't think he's had time to write a report."

"No. No. Of course not." Mr. McCormick looked flustered. "It's just fifteen miles to Fort Malden. I can saddle my horse and be there in a couple of hours. Colonel Maitland will see me. He'll tell me what's happened to my boys." He pressed his fingers to his forehead, as if trying to order his thoughts. "But Maitland must have been up all night crossing the ice to Pelee Island . . . then fighting a battle . . . then marching his army back to Fort Malden. If he's not already asleep in his bed, he will be by the time I get there. So that won't do." He shook his head. "It will be tomorrow before we have word about our sons. What am I going to tell Mary?"

All this time Mr. McCormick was paying no attention to me. What could I do to bring his attention to such a trifle as a bunch of stolen jewellery? I reached for the top buttons of my coat, thinking *at least I can make him look at it.* As soon as I had enough buttons undone, I flung open the neck of my coat. Words tumbled out of my mouth. "Sir, I didn't just come to tell you about the battle. I've brought some jewellery that belongs to you. I'm sure it belongs to you. Please look!"

He looked. For a moment he did not seem to comprehend what was right before his eyes: the rings, the locket, the string of pearls, the rope of jet beads and the little gold cross.

"See! I rescued them for you."

"That's my mother's jewellery!" From the look on Mr. McCormick's face, you'd think he'd been shot.

"There's more! Let me show you the rest!" I pulled up my coat sleeves so he could see the bracelets on my wrists, and then I reached into my pockets for the brooches. There were

about a dozen brooches, enamel, ivory, gemstones in fancy
settings.

He stared from the brooches in my hands to the bracelets on
my wrists back to the necklaces around my neck. At last I had
his attention! He looked straight into my eyes. "Who are you?"

"Theodore Dickson," I answered, thinking that 'Theodore'
sounded more grown-up and responsible than 'Dory'.

"Where did you get this jewellery?"

"From the thief who stole it. I think he broke into your
house on Pelee Island. He dropped those things when he was
running away. I was chasing him."

"So you stopped your pursuit and picked them up?"

"Not exactly." I began to sweat. *I must explain this better
or Mr. McCormick will suspect me of doing something wrong.* I
gulped nervously. "It's a long story."

"This is beyond belief. My mother never told me that her
jewellery was missing. I can't imagine her leaving it behind."
He shook his head. "Wait here!" Then he charged off to another
part of the house, leaving me with my hands full of brooches.
In a minute he returned, carrying a wooden bowl that he must
have fetched from the kitchen.

"Put everything in the bowl. I'll take you to meet my mother
and the rest of my family. They're in the parlour. You can tell
your story to all of us together."

"That's what I want to do." I dumped the brooches into the
bowl. The bracelets followed, and then the long rope of jet
beads. As I undid the clasps of the necklaces, I said, "But first,
I must look after my horse. She's tied to your hitching post outside in the cold. She's just carried me here from Pelee Island.
Have you room in your barn? She needs resting for an hour
before we go on."

No longer flustered, he said, "Surely you don't plan to travel
farther tonight?"

"To Albertville."

"Another twelve miles! That won't do! If your horse has come
all the way from Pelee Island over the ice, she needs food and

water as well as rest. I'll have a servant take her to the stable.
You'll be staying here tonight."

When I was adding the rest of the jewellery to the heap in
the bowl, the rings all slid off the locket's delicate silver chain.
Carrying the bowl, Mr. McCormick led the way. The room
where he took me was filled with people, young and old. They
lounged about in armchairs and on sofas upholstered in dark
red plush. In an armchair next to the fireplace sat an old lady.
Her dress was black, and her hair was silvery. There was also
a middle-aged lady, likely Mr. McCormick's wife, as well as a
young man who might be their son. The family included a boy
around my age, four girls of different sizes, two small boys, and
a baby in a cradle. Everybody (except the baby) looked up and
stared when we entered. We must have been an odd sight—Mr.
McCormick carrying the wooden bowl, followed by me, with the
red scarf around my middle and my coonskin hat in my hand.

Mr. McCormick marched up to the old lady and lowered the
bowl to let her see the contents. When she looked into the bowl,
her face turned white, and then red. Others crowded around
her, peering to see what was in the bowl. The old lady said, "I
packed all this in my jewellery box before we fled. I set it on
my bed for the maid to carry to the sleigh. There was such confusion and such hurry to escape that she forgot to bring it."
The old lady picked up one of the bracelets and looked at it. "I
hoped that everything would still be there when we returned.
I didn't mention my loss to anybody. Telling you would just
have caused more worry."

Cries of, "Oh, Grandmother!" came from all sides. "You should
have told us!"

She put the bracelet back and plucked a ring from the bowl.
It was the least brilliant of all the jewels, a gold band set with
pearls and tiny red stones. She put it on one of her fingers. As
she turned her hand this way and that to inspect it, tears ran
down her furrowed cheeks. "This ring was my husband's first
gift to me." Then she looked in my direction. "Who is our visitor? I presume he has something to do with this."

Mr. McCormick said, "His name Theodore Dickson. I don't know the whole story, but somehow he rescued the jewellery—'rescued' is the word he used—and thought it must belong to our family."

"Because we're the only family on Pelee Island wealthy enough to own it," the old lady said drily. "Well, Theodore, take off your coat and let us hear your story."

Mr. McCormick cleared his throat. "Before he does, there is something important I must tell you." He cleared his throat again. Now he had everyone's attention. "This morning there was a battle. Colonel Maitland's army has driven the invaders from Pelee Island."

A chorus of voices. "Thank God!"

"Were my brothers in it?"

"Are the boys safe?"

Mr. McCormick said grimly, "I don't know." He paused. "Colonel Maitland is sure to send me a report as soon as possible. Theodore witnessed the battle. He will tell us what he saw." Now he turned toward me. "I must introduce my family before you begin. You'll be joining us for dinner, Theodore, and spending the night here. I want you to feel welcome."

I had taken off my coat, and now I stood in front of the fireplace, facing the family. The old lady's armchair was close by, and the wooden bowl was on her lap. From the corner of my eye, I saw her pick up and examine one piece of jewellery after another while Mr. McCormick was introducing his family. His mother's name was Elizabeth; his wife's was Mary. The young man was their oldest son, Alexander. I don't remember the names of the others. They all (except the baby) said they were pleased to meet me. Then I began my story.

"I'd spent the night in the loft of Adam Bruner's barn at the southern tip of the island. When I woke up in the morning, I looked out the window. There was a long line of redcoats—about one hundred men—stretched out on the ice. Then a big crowd of Patriot soldiers came running out from the shore.

Their officers formed them up in two lines. The Patriots fired first. The redcoats fired back. The Patriots returned that volley. Then the redcoats fixed their bayonets and charged. After taking one look at those bayonets, the Patriot soldiers turned tail and ran for their lives. I watched all this through the window of the loft.

"After the battle was over, I didn't leave the loft right away. It was a while later that I looked out the window again and saw a man carrying a box under his arm. He walked like he was in a hurry, heading north across the ice. This looked strange. I wondered what he was doing. When he stopped and looked around, he was close enough for me to see his face. I recognized him. His name's Peter Dash. I'd seen him cheat at cards. I'd heard him brag about his schemes for getting rich. From everything I knew about him, I figured he must be up to something crooked, carrying that box under his arm. I didn't want him get away with more deviltry. So I climbed down from the loft and chased after him.

"I was catching up to him when he came to a bad place where the ice cracked open. He fell through. I fished him out of the water and took him back to Pelee Island and left him at Bruner's house. He'd dropped the box before he fell into the water. When the box hit the ice, it burst open and the jewellery spilled out. So after I'd rescued the man, I went back and rescued the jewellery. I knew your family had left Pelee Island before the invasion and gone to your house in Colchester. So I came straight here."

That was all I had to say. As soon as I finished speaking, they started talking to each other, mostly about the three brothers who were with Colonel Maitland's army. The old lady had been trying on the rings. Now she lifted her head and looked at me. "One ring is missing," she said. "My emerald ring."

"I . . . I brought all the rings that were there." Was she accusing me? The jewellery box had been furnished with little slots for rings. Back there on the ice, when I took the seven rings from their slots, I had noticed that the eighth slot was empty. The rings had all fit snugly into their slots. Still, it was possible that one ring could have jolted loose, fallen out and slid across the ice and fallen into the water. I was close to tears, thinking that Mrs. McCormick suspected me of stealing her emerald ring.

She must have seen my dismay. "Theodore, don't think for a moment that I blame you. I have nothing but gratitude for what you have done. We'll say no more about the missing ring."

I let out a deep breath, vastly relieved to hear this. But I still wondered what had happened to her emerald ring.

CHAPTER THIRTY-ONE

I expected that the family would have plenty of questions to ask me. But they were too worried about the three brothers to care much about the jewellery, or about the man who stole it, or about me. After I'd told them about the battle, they were busy talking with one another about John, William and David, holding hands, hugging, and assuring each other that the boys would be fine. I took a seat by the fire, ignored. I was an outsider, a stranger. Yet I could imagine how they felt, having lost my own two brothers, Andrew and Alexander, lying in their graves back home.

After a while, a maid came into the room to announce that dinner was ready to be served. "We have a guest," Mr. McCormick told her, "You need to set another place."

"Give me a minute," the maid said grumpily. On her face was an expression of annoyance aimed at me.

We waited to give her time to set my place, and then we filed into the dining room. The meal began with soup. When the soup bowls were cleared away, the maid brought roast beef, potatoes, carrots and bread and butter. Then came apple pie, cheese and tea. This was the first food I'd eaten in more than twenty-four hours. I was too busy eating to have much to say.

In fact, nobody talked much during the meal. There was little conversation beyond "Please pass the butter," and similar requests. The McCormicks barely nibbled at the food. After dinner, Mary McCormick told the maid to make up a bedroom for me. I was dog-tired, but before going to bed, I went out to the stable to make sure that Labelle was comfortable. One of the servants had given her food and water. I rubbed her down before returning to the house. That night I slept in a warm bedroom with a down-filled pillow under my head.

At breakfast the next morning, I knew from their puffy eyes that no one in the family had slept as well as I. Beyond a polite "Good morning," nobody had much to say. On the table were serving plates of bacon and eggs and fried potatoes. I filled my plate and tried to eat slowly because I'd feel embarrassed to be gobbling up a big breakfast while others barely touched their food.

Mr. McCormick broke the silence, "We'll hear soon. Colonel Maitland won't keep us waiting. A messenger must already be on his way." The clock on the dining room sideboard read eight o'clock. It was still too early for a messenger to arrive.

Yet only a few minutes later, there was a knock on the door. No one moved. There was no rush of people from the table. They seemed to dread hearing the news that they had been so anxiously waiting for. Then Mr. McCormick pushed back his chair and stood up. That was the signal for other chairs to scrape back. Except for me, old Mrs. Elizabeth McCormick was the only person who did not rush to the door. She sat for a moment, head bowed, before she stood up slowly and joined the others. I left the table also, but waited to one side.

In the open doorway stood a young officer. He wore a grey greatcoat and a tall hat with a plume. His cheeks were pink from the cold, and his eyes were bright. From the quivering at the corners of his mouth, I thought he was trying not to smile.

"Mr. McCormick," he began, "I am Ensign Charles Lester. I serve as aide to Colonel Maitland. He is at the moment writing his official report. But he didn't want to keep you waiting for this news. Yesterday we drove the invaders from Pelee Island. Colonel Maitland particularly asked me to tell you that your sons are heroes and that all three are safe."

There was a low sound like a soft wind as all the McCormicks let out their breath at the same time. "Thanks be to God," murmured old Mrs. McCormick.

The younger Mrs. McCormick burst into tears, "I knew they'd be safe," she sobbed, which showed me that she had been expecting the worst.

"Come in!" said Mr. McCormick. "Take off your coat and make yourself comfortable. That young fellow—he pointed at me—witnessed the battle and the rout of the Patriot army. That's all he saw. You can tell us the whole story."

He helped Ensign Lester out of his greatcoat, took his hat, and led him into the big, comfortable room where the family had gathered the day before. A warm fire crackled on the hearth. Lester stood with his back to the fireplace, facing everyone, just as I had stood the day before to tell my story. The door from the dining room was open, and I saw the maid standing in the doorway, her head cocked, ready to hear whatever Lester was about to say. She glanced about and then slipped into the room on tiptoe.

"I'll start at the beginning," said Lester. "Early in the week, Colonel Maitland received word that Pelee Island had been invaded by a Patriot army from Ohio. He sent out men to test the ice. When they reported that it was a foot-and-a-half thick, he decided it was safe to cross with an army. He ordered up four companies of the Thirty-second Regiment, one company of the Eighty-third regiment, a detachment of cavalry from St. Thomas, one company of Essex volunteers and a small group of Indian warriors. We had two cannons with us—six-pounders—but we never used them. That was Friday, the day before yesterday. We took up a position on the lakeshore, facing in the direction of Pelee Island. We lit fires to keep ourselves warm, and there we ate and rested—horses and men—until two o'clock in the morning. Then we set out across the ice in sleighs" —Lester paused dramatically, his glance sweeping from face to face until every member of the family was holding their breath with anticipation— "expertly guided by David and William McCormick."

Lester waited until his audience had finished cheering before he continued. "Frankly, I don't know how they did it, because the night was black as pitch. But when the sun came up, there we were, just offshore at the north end of Pelee Island."

"Saturday, the third of March," said Mr. McCormick. "I want to get this straight."

"That is correct." Lester paused. "Colonel Maitland had his strategy planned. He knew his force of five hundred men could make a clean sweep of Pelee Island. But he would not be satisfied just to drive out the invaders and let them escape back to Sandusky. No, sir! He wanted to capture those scalawags and march them to Fort Malden as prisoners of war.

"So Colonel Maitland divided his army into three divisions. He sent Captain George Brown with two companies of the Thirty-second Regiment—ninety men—with William McCormick as their guide, down the west side of the Island to Mosquito Bay at the southern tip. Then he ordered the cavalry—twenty men under Captain Ermatinger's command—to circle south along the east side. So he had cavalry and infantry waiting to intercept any invaders trying to escape back to Ohio.

"Now Colonel Maitland was ready to send his main force to engage in battle with the enemy. 'Do I have volunteers to lead the charge?' he asked, and at once Captain John McCormick dismounted from his horse and flourished his sword."

The family cheered, "Hurray for John!"

Lester waited for silence before continuing. "We went ashore expecting a battle, but the Patriot army was already running away. We chased those rascals right through the island, from north to south, where Captain Brown's division and the cavalry were waiting for them. Brown had formed his men in one long line in open order, positioned one-and-one-half paces apart.

"The Patriot soldiers streamed out of the woods with us at

their heels. There was Captain Brown with his men lined up across the ice, the cavalry on their flank. Now the battle began. There might have been a real fight, because the Patriot army had a couple of first-class officers. But right at the beginning, both were shot dead."

Lester's words took me back to the battle. I remembered Captain Van Rensselaer and Major Hoadley rallying their men. I remembered the fire spurting from gun barrels, and the smoke, and the bodies on the blood-stained ice.

Lester was still talking. "After a few volleys, Brown's detachment fixed their bayonets and charged. I saw young William McCormick in the thick of it—"

More cheers from the family!

"As soon as the Patriot soldiers saw those blades coming at them, they scattered in every direction. Our cavalry chased them until Captain Ermatinger's horse had its foot go through the ice. Then the cavalry wheeled away rather than continue the pursuit over thin ice. So some of the enemy escaped.

"That's how it ended. We went back over the island, searching every house and barn, the woods and the swamp for Patriot soldiers. We scoured the island until we were sure we'd shot or captured every single one. Then we loaded the wounded onto sleighs to return to Fort Malden, taking with us our prisoners of war. We were back at Fort Malden last night. The whole operation had taken only thirty hours."

Silence greeted the end of Lester's speech. After a few moments, Mr. McCormick asked, "How many casualties?"

"On our side? We estimate twenty-eight of Captain Brown's infantry were injured. One died on the way back to Fort Malden. One cavalry man was killed. As for enemy casualties, the two command officers were killed, as well as a good number of soldiers, both in the battle and during our sweep of the island."

Mr. McCormick rubbed his hands together. "Thank you, Ensign Lester, for this wonderful news. Now that you've had your exercise this morning, please join us for breakfast. We had started eating when you arrived. The food will be cold, but there's plenty of it." As he spoke, the maid slipped out of the room.

"I'll be glad to join you, Sir," said Lester, looking pleased with himself.

I'd already had enough breakfast. I reckoned that as soon as I'd fed and watered Labelle, I'd come back to the house to thank the McCormicks for their hospitality. That's when I'd bring up the subject of old Mrs. McCormick's jewellery. Mr. McCormick might need reminding about that. I hoped that his joy at learning that his sons were safe would inspire his generosity when it came to thanking me.

CHAPTER THIRTY-TWO

abelle welcomed my attention. As well as giving her food and water, I gave her a good brushing. "We'll be leaving soon," I told her. "It's a beautiful sunny day, and you have no sled to pull." She nickered softly when I left, her eyes showing her disappointment that we were not setting forth that very moment.

I felt sure that Mr. McCormick would want to reward me for restoring his mother's jewellery. At the same time, I was a bit worried that he might have his own suspicions about the emerald ring. It was Sunday morning. The Colchester church bell was ringing. When I entered the house, I found that Ensign Lester had already left, returning to Fort Malden. The McCormick family was getting ready to attend church. With the exception of Mr. McCormick, they were putting on their coats and hats. Mr. McCormick stood beside his wife, who was fastening the clasp of her hood. He gave me a nod when he saw me enter and motioned me to approach.

Stepping around several children who were sitting on the floor pulling on their boots, I made my way to him. "Theodore," he said, "I need to have a word with you." He turned to his wife, "Mary, go on without me. I'll join you at the service as soon as I've had a chance to thank Theodore as he deserves."

She smiled. "Thank him generously, my dear."

Those kind words melted away the last of my worries as Mr. McCormick led me along the hall to his study, where he told me to take a chair. His study had wood-panelled walls and a big desk with lots of drawers and cubby-holes. Instead of sitting down at the desk, he pulled up a chair and sat facing me. He got straight to the point. "Theodore, words of thanks aren't enough to repay you for what you've done. You might have kept the jewellery and found a buyer who wouldn't ask awkward questions. I appreciate your honesty. You deserve a reward."

I held my breath. I think he was waiting for me to say something, but I was tongue-tied with suspense. After a few moments he said, "One hundred dollars is about the right amount, wouldn't you say?"

"Yes, Sir," I let out my breath. One hundred dollars! That was more than enough to replace old Prince. I could buy a milk cow, too, and a piglet to fatten up for next winter's eating. One hundred dollars meant I wouldn't need to look for work at towns along the Talbot Road. I could go home right now. As soon as the snow melted and the ground thawed, I could be out there ploughing the fields.

"Thank you, Sir." I mumbled, barely able to speak.

Mr. McCormick went to his desk, opened a drawer and pulled out a sheaf of banknotes half an inch thick. I'd never before seen so much money at one time. He counted out ten bills, each for ten dollars, drawn on The Bank of Upper Canada. Then he rummaged in a different drawer, where he found a canvas pocket attached to a cloth belt. He put the banknotes into the pocket. "Take off your shirt," he said, "and put on this money belt. Wear it next to your skin. That's the safest place to carry money."

I didn't like to take off my shirt, because then he might notice how shabby it was. But I did what he told me to do. When I had my shirt back on, I sat down again. He now asked me friendly questions about myself, such as where I came from and what brought me to this part of the country.

"I come from Niagara," I told him. "My plan was to look for work in one of the settlements along the Talbot Road."

"What took you over to Pelee Island at the very time when

most people who live there had left to seek safety on the mainland?"

This was a question I had been expecting. "I'd been staying at the home of Jacob Fox in Gosfield Township. He needed me to take a message to Adam Bruner. There was a patch of bad ice just off Pelee Island's northwest point. My horse and I went through. We made it safely to shore. We were wet and cold, so we stopped for help at the first house we came to. It was George's Fox's home."

"Ah!" said Mr. McCormick. "George's house isn't far from our place on Pelee Island. We live on the north bay, partway between George's house on the northwest corner and the lighthouse on Brushy Marsh Point. I warned George and his brothers to take their families over to the mainland, just as I took mine. They told me they'd rather stay on the island to defend their property."

Mr. McCormick didn't seem to know that George Fox had a brother who supported the rebellion. Nor did he know about the Patriots' promise not to harm Jacob's brothers or their property. A promise not kept. But none of this was information that I should share with William McCormick. I liked Jacob Fox's family and didn't want to make trouble for them.

"I think George and his brothers made a mistake by staying." Mr. McCormick shook his head. "As for you, Theodore, since you're looking for work, I'll be happy to write you a reference to help you find suitable employment."

"Sir, I appreciate that. But the only reason I was looking for work was to help my family. Thanks to your generosity, I won't have to do that. One hundred dollars is enough for all of our needs. I'm going home as fast as I can."

"I understand that feeling." He leaned back in his chair. "I'm anxious to take my family back to Pelee Island. It's not safe yet. There'll be at least one more attempt to invade Canada before it's over. But sooner or later, all the trouble along the border will be over."

"I hope so, Sir."

"It will be, because President Van Buren doesn't want a war with England. Trade between the United States and Britain is too important. Unfortunately, many people in the United States believe that the American Revolution won't be over until they've annexed Canada. They failed when they tried in 1812. Now they're trying again—all fired up by that maniac William Lyon Mackenzie. Now that his revolution in Toronto has failed, he's down there in the States telling Americans that thousands of Canadians want their support to throw off British rule."

I listened patiently, just as I had earlier listened patiently to Duncan Fraser lecture me from the opposite side.

"Americans talk about liberty Their Constitution says that all men are created equal. But they have thousands of Black Americans existing in a condition of slavery. How equal is that? Whereas, slavery was abolished throughout the British Empire five years ago—" He stopped abruptly. "Sorry, Theodore. Excuse my rhetoric. I'm a politician, you know. Former Member of Parliament for Essex County. My family say I constantly forget that I'm not making a speech in the Legislature." He paused. "There's one more thing we need to talk about." Mr. McCormick's brows came together in a frown. "I am a magistrate. The administration of justice falls under my authority. A crime has been committed. A thief broke into my house and stole personal property. The fact that it was my house rather than that of another person is neither here nor there. It isn't good enough that the property has been restored. The thief must be brought to justice."

"How can I help?"

"You told us his name."

"Peter Dash."

"You also told us that after you saved his life you took him to Adam Bruner's house. Do you think he's still there?"

"No, Sir. I'm sure he'd leave as soon as he was warmed up and his clothes dried. He's probably left the island already."

"Have you any idea where he would go.? You seem to know quite a bit about him."

"I'll tell you everything I know. When I first met Dash, he worked at the sawmill in Anthony's Mills, near Fort Erie. As it happens, I spent a night at the home of Mr. and Mrs. Goodwin in Fort Erie."

"Leonard Goodwin is a good friend of mine. Go on."

"The Goodwins' granddaughter Laura lives with them."

"I know about that. The Goodwins' daughter married into a wealthy Toronto family. She and her husband both died in the cholera epidemic of 1832. They had one child, Laura. It was a terrible tragedy. Leonard and his wife have raised Laura since she was ten years old. She must be quite a young lady by now."

"Yes. She's beautiful!" I hesitated. "Well, I spent one night at the Goodwins' home in Fort Erie. When Laura learned that my next stop was going to be Anthony's Mills, she asked me to take a letter to a friend who lived there. I agreed to do so. The friend turned out to be Peter Dash. It was a love letter."

"Are you saying the Goodwins' granddaughter writes love letters to a labourer in a sawmill! Do they know about this?"

"They don't know anything about it. What's worse is that she wants to run away with him. Dash is a fortune hunter. With my own ears, I heard him tell a friend that he's going to marry her because she's rich. Even before I knew he was a thief, I thought somebody ought to warn her. I think he'll find Laura as soon as he can and run away with her."

"She must be warned."

"I'm going to stop in Fort Erie on my way home to Niagara. to tell her everything—how he cheats at cards and how he stole the jewellery. If I need to, I'll tell her grandparents, too."

"Leave it to me to tell the Goodwins. I'll write to Leonard. I'll also write to the local magistrate. Like me, he has the authority to perform marriages. We can't let this Dash fellow trick her into marriage to gain control of her fortune—and I expect it's a considerable fortune that her father left her. I'll also write to the Chief Constable in Fort Erie to ask him to assign a constable to the case."

Mr. McCormick gave me a stern look. "Theodore, you must go to the Goodwins' home as soon as you can. Warn Laura. If Dash shows up in Fort Erie, you'll be able to identify him. After we've caught the fellow and arraigned him, you'll be a key witness at the trial."

"I can do that. I need to make one stop in Albertville. After that, I'll make my way to Fort Erie as fast as I can. Even if Dash goes there directly, I can get there first. I have a good horse. Labelle can cover two hundred miles in a week." Relief flooded through me, knowing that now it wouldn't be up to me alone to stop Laura from marrying Peter Dash.

Mr. McCormick stood up. "I must hurry to join my family at church. This is certainly a day for giving thanks to the Lord." He cleared his throat. "And you too must be on your way."

CHAPTER THIRTY-THREE

$\mathcal{S}$now had fallen during the night, but now the sky was clear. The new snow slid off the trees. and lay in little heaps under the branches. I felt spring in the air. The Talbot Road was thronged with sleighs carrying people home from church. Sleigh bells jingle-jangled, and folks waved to me as I rode by.

I had to reach Fort Erie before Peter Dash did in order to prevent him from marrying Laura . . . if this was his plan. I was also needed in Fort Erie to identify Dash . . . if the local constable arrested him for the theft of old Mrs. McCormick's jewellery. If . . . if . . . the uncertainty troubled me.

What troubled me even more was losing the chance to spend some time visiting Jacob Fox's family before I returned to Chippawa. Although I dreaded telling Jacob what had happened to the load of muskets, I had hoped to sit down to dinner with the family, and then play a friendly game of whist. I'd looked forward to talking with Anna about books or poetry or anything that she wanted to talk about. As Labelle and I jogged along, I pictured Anna in my mind—her smooth light brown hair, the amused smile that sometimes lifted the corners of her mouth, the large brown eyes that looked right at you. I had thought of visiting for a couple of days. Now this would be impossible. A couple of hours was all the time I could afford to stay.

When I reached Jacob Fox's house, the family had just returned from the church in Albertville. Mrs. Fox, Sarah and Anna were hanging up their long cloaks on hooks inside the kitchen door. Anna's hair was coiled into a fancy knot on top of her head, which made her look more grown-up than fourteen. From the warm look in her eyes, I thought she was happy to see me. The three boys were pulling off their stiff-looking Sunday coats. Jacob was not there.

"We've been worried about you," said Mrs. Fox. "My husband said you were making a delivery for him. We expected you back two days ago. Jacob will be glad to see you. He's out in the barn, putting our horse in its stall."

"I'll take my horse there now," I said. The family had not seen Labelle standing outside. No harness. No sled. Before anything else, I had to tell Jacob in private about the muskets and the battle.

I led Labelle to the barn. Jacob was latching the stall door after brushing his horse. He took one look at me "Well? What happened?"

"The sled went through the ice just before we reached Pelee Island. I cut the traces, as you told me to do. I saved the horse, but the sled and the muskets are at the bottom of Lake Erie. When we made it to shore, the first house we came to was your brother George's place. He took us in. That's his saddle on my horse."

"I heard at church about the battle," said Jacob. "From all accounts, the muskets wouldn't have made much difference."

"Likely not. The Patriot army didn't have many real soldiers. Most of the men were there to loot. They took over your brother's house at gunpoint, telling him he'd have to supply lodging for twenty men."

"What!" Jacob's face turned white. "I was given a solemn promise that my brothers and their property would be left alone."

"That's what George told them. But that promise did him no good. They tied him to a chair. They slaughtered his hogs. They brought in a barrel of rum they'd stolen from Squire McCormick's house. After they'd been drinking for four hours, a brawl broke out. That's when I had a chance to sneak away."

"Dammit!" Jacob exploded. "How can I make it up to George?" His face reddened and his voice sputtered with anger. "If the Patriot army did that to George, then Henry and John may have been molested too. I'll go over to Pelee Island tomorrow to see about it. There are some other men I need to talk to as well. If we're ever going to achieve reform in this province, we can't give up now. As for you, I suppose you're on your way back to Chippawa."

"I'd hoped to stay here for a short visit, but a problem came up that I need to take care of. So I'll be leaving as soon as I've rested my horse."

"When you've fed her, join us for a meal before you go. My family think I sent you to Olinda with a load of firewood. That's the story I gave them. There's an iron foundry in Olinda that sometimes runs out of fuel for the smelter."

Jacob's wide shoulders were stooped as he left the barn, a disappointed man. I didn't entirely agree with his goals and certainly not with the Patriots' methods, but I had sympathy, just the same.

Mrs. Fox, Sarah and Anna had food already on the table when I returned to the house. Bacon and eggs and pancakes with maple syrup—boiled down from sap just the day before, they told me. Mrs. Fox and the girls seemed sorry I was leaving so soon. Anna said she had a book that she wanted to give me.

After we had eaten, Anna asked me to sit down at the little table in the sitting room where she had been reading *Gulliver's Travels* the day I first arrived. "I'll fetch the book I want to give you," she said, and she left the room. In a couple of minutes she returned, carrying a book. It had a blue cloth cover, with the title *Tales from Shakespeare* stamped in gold letters. She placed the book on the table and then placed her hand over it as if to say, *You can't have it yet.* Then she levelled her eyes at me and said softly, "You didn't go to Olinda, did you?"

With her clear brown eyes looking straight into mine, there was no way I could lie. "No. I didn't go to Olinda."

"When I heard at church this morning that there had been a battle on Pelee Island, I felt sure that's where Vati sent you."

"The battle wasn't on the island. It was fought on the ice, off the island's southern tip. I watched it from the loft of a barn. It was horrible."

She leaned forward and lowered her vice to a whisper. "I'm glad the Patriots lost. Vati thinks I don't know what's going on in the world. He thinks women and girls are better off not to know. But that newspaper he reads, *The Constitution*, I read every copy he brings into the house." I was so startled to hear this that I didn't know what to say. "It's published by William Lyon Mackenzie," said Anna. "And that's not the only thing by Mackenzie that I've read. I've read his *Report on Grievances*, too."

"I know about Mackenzie's *Report on Grievances*," I said. "I read about it in a copy of *The Constitution* that I saw in the public room of an inn where I stayed one night. The newspaper said it was 570 pages long."

"I haven't read the whole thing," she admitted, "but I've read enough to know that the situation in Upper Canada is very bad. The Family Compact hogs all the important jobs for themselves, so that one man gets the salary for three or four positions. Unless you're a son or nephew of somebody in the Family you have no chance of ever getting ahead." She took a quick breath. "What gives me hope is knowing that old King William read the *Report on Grievances* and prodded the British government to set matters straight in Upper Canada."

"King William has been dead for more than a year," I objected.

"Of course I know that! But Queen Victoria is already taking steps to deal with the problems. She's sending somebody to Canada to investigate and tell her what needs to be done. A change in the way we're governed makes more sense than starting a war, where people get killed or driven from their homes."

"I agree." I gazed at her, confounded to hear a girl talk like this. "I mean, that's what I think, too."

Anna smiled. "Now I'm going to tell you about this book I'm giving you." She lifted her hand, which had been covering it, and shoved the book across the table toward me. "It's a collection of stories that Charles Lamb and his sister took from Shakespeare's plays. Not all the plays. Just comedies and tragedies. They're lovely stories."

I picked up the book and opened it. There was a list of more than a dozen titles. "Which is your favourite?"

"'The Tempest'. It's about a girl named Miranda. She's my age. When she was a baby, she and her father were cast upon an island."

"Like Pelee Island?"

"About the same size, I think."

"I'll read that story first."

"Then you must write to me and tell me what you think of it."

I didn't know what to say. I'd never written anyone a letter in my entire life. But Anna didn't seem to understand my hesitation. "There's a post office in Albertville," she said, "with postal service three times a week. I can check every Saturday, when we go in for the farmers' market."

"Fine!" I said. "That's what I'll do."

We rose from the table and went back to the kitchen. I carried the book with me.

Mrs. Fox brought me my bundle, which held my small clothes, my Sunday shirt, and my brush and comb. "These are the things you left here when you went to Olinda," she said. "My husband tells me that you've got rid of the sled and are riding your horse back to Chippawa. May I offer you a saddlebag? It will be easier than carrying a bundle on a stick."

Then she gave me a stout canvas saddlebag, into which I packed everything, including the book. Anna watched me pack. I wished that I could be alone with her for a few minutes. But then, I wouldn't know what to do or say. So it was just as well that we weren't alone.

I went out to the barn to saddle Labelle. When I was ready to leave, I went back to the house to say goodbye. Everyone came outdoors into the sunshine to wave as I rode away.

CHAPTER THIRTY-FOUR

We were going at a steady pace, sharing the Talbot Road with sleighs full of people enjoying a Sunday afternoon drive. The snow was crunchy. The willow trees were golden green, waiting for the first warm day for them to put forth their leaves. I was thinking about Anna and wishing I was book-learned like her. Reading those Shakespeare stories was bound to help. After I'd finished reading "The Tempest" I'd write her a letter. Even though I'd been done school for a year; maybe Mr. Pringle my old schoolmaster would help me with it. But he'd be disappointed that I hadn't learned enough—or had confidence enough—to write my own letter. I hoped I would like the stories Anna gave me. I could see Anna's brown eyes looking straight at me. She wouldn't want me to say I liked the stories if I really didn't.

Anna wasn't the only girl I thought about. There was Laura, too. I had a strong feeling that Peter Dash would waste no time making her his wife. If all went well, I could reach the Goodwins' home in Fort Erie in a week. How long would it take Peter Dash?

Twilight brought me to the farm where I had stayed after leaving Morpeth on my way to Albertville. I stopped there again. The house was crowded with children—a round dozen of them, mostly twins, and none more than ten years old. The farmer's wife was a lean tired-looking woman with a belly on her that looked as though she'd swallowed a pumpkin. Soon there'd be another child, or maybe two.

The farmer showed no more interest in politics than he had on my previous visit, when we had talked about crop failures. He didn't know about the battle on the ice at Pelee Island until I told him about it. My description of the slaughter of George Fox's hogs made him clench his fists and curse the men who did it.

Three of the children had to give up the bed they shared in order to provide me with a place to sleep. They crawled into other beds with other children. I thought about Anna and wanted to read the story she'd told me was her favourite, but with that swarm of children in the same room with me, this was not the right time or place.

When I was about to leave in the morning, I offered the farmer one dollar in payment for lodging me and my horse. He said not to bother, that it was a pleasure to help a friend of Sam Kemp, because Mr. Kemp had helped him out once, a long time ago. When he refused the money, his wife gave him such an icy stare that he changed his mind.

In Morpeth I stopped at the tavern where I had previously stayed. Mr. Little, the elegant tavern keeper with his colourful black and red vest and black tie, remembered me. "You're the lad who told me about the blazing ship that didn't go over Niagara Falls," he said. He was affable and welcoming, but made clear that this time I would be a paying guest. His friendship with Sam Kemp no longer meant free lodging for me and my horse.

Mr. Little had heard about the failure of the invasion of Pelee Island. He brought up the subject after joining me for a pint of ale at a table in the public room, the room where I had sat chatting with him and Duncan Fraser one month ago.

"Our friend Mr. Fraser has not been back," he said. He was observing me carefully, his expression like that of a hungry cat watching a mouse hole. When I did not answer, Mr. Little leaned forward and said in a low voice, "There was a secret society that used to meet in my tavern from time to time. They will not be meeting here again. Do you understand my meaning?"

I nodded. Mr. Little no longer supported the rebellion. He had changed his mind.

I rode away early in the morning. Before noon, I passed the small log house where Ralph Butler and his wife Miranda lived. It was a hard wrench for me to ride on by without stopping to say hello. But I knew that if I paid Ralph and Miranda a visit, they'd keep me there the rest of the day and all night. I wished that I could tell Ralph that I had visited his beloved Pelee Island and had seen the lighthouse that he had painted. But if I wanted to reach Fort Erie before Peter Dash got there, I had no time to lose.

Miranda Butler had the same name as the girl in Anna's favourite story. I hadn't read it yet. I could have read it the night before, in my room at the tavern in Morpeth. But I was beginning to like the idea that it was waiting, safe in the saddlebag, for me to take out and read at the right time.

I avoided Mrs. Hoover's comfortable home in Williamsville as well, but for a different reason. Mrs. Hoover, with her magnified all-seeing eyes behind her thick spectacles, was the aunt of Mr. Kemp's departed wife. Mrs. Hoover had been surprised to hear that her niece owned a loom and spinning wheel. Of course, she had not known about them! They never existed. It had all been trickery. If I'd been smarter, I'd have figured that out for myself.

I liked Mrs. Hoover, who was so kind and ladylike. I liked her fat old horses, Pagan and Slow Poke. Labelle liked them, too. And Mrs. Hoover's housemaid Vera liked me. She must have liked me a great deal, because when I was leaving, Vera had said, "You may kiss me if you like." I was curious to know whether she would repeat this invitation. Vera was pretty, with grey-green eyes and pink cheeks. But when I thought about kissing Vera, I saw Anna's serious face and big brown eyes. It made me feel ashamed even to be tempted. So I stayed for the night at an inn outside Williamsville, spending another dollar of the one hundred dollars that Mr. McCormick had given me as my reward.

CHAPTER THIRTY-FIVE

hree days later I rode up to the Goodwins' elegant, two-storey home. I dismounted, tied Labelle's rein to the hitching post, and knocked at the front door. It opened after the first rap, and there stood Laura. She was wearing a full-length, deep purple hooded cloak. On her hands were fine kidskin gloves, and on her feet were black leather ankle boots with brass buckles. Not quite covering her golden curls was a tiny white veil no bigger than a lace handkerchief.

"Oh!" Laura exclaimed. "I was just going out." Her eyebrows lifted. "I remember you! Last month you delivered a letter for me. That was very kind of you." A tiny frown appeared between her delicate brows. "I'm sorry, but I don't remember your name."

"Dory. I'm Dory Dickson. I need to speak to you. Is there someplace where we won't be interrupted?"

"Well, I *am* in a hurry. But let me hear what you have to say. My grandparents aren't home, and the maid is in the kitchen. Nobody's going to interrupt us if we talk right here." She motioned me inside and closed the door. "What is it you need to tell me?"

Gulping nervously, I pulled off my coonskin hat. "What I must tell you is not easy to say. I mean . . . you're such a desirable young lady. Even if you were as poor as a church mouse, there must be a hundred men who would want to marry you." Her frown deepened. "That is to say . . . it wouldn't be just for your money. You are so beautiful!"

Her frown disappeared, and a soft look came into her eyes. She reached out and patted my arm. "Poor Dory! I don't know what I've done to make you feel this way. You're just a boy. Maybe you think you're in love with me, but—"

"I didn't come to tell you that!" My face must have turned as red as a beet. "I came here to warn you about the man you wrote that letter to. Peter Dash. He's a cheater. A thief. A fortune hunter."

She lifted her hand from my arm. "Peter is none of those things." Her soft expression turned to one of utter fury. "Peter Dash is a gentleman, and I am soon to be his wife. This is my engagement ring!"

She pulled off the glove from her left hand. On the fourth finger was an emerald ring.

The emerald was round in shape, and the same size as the fingernail of my little finger. Tiny gold hooks clasped it to its base. The emerald was as green as new grass and as full of light as sunshine through clear water.

"He stole that ring!"

"How dare you!"

"Listen! This is what I came to tell you. I've been on Pelee Island. I saw him there. He broke into Squire McCormick's house when it was empty. He stole old Mrs. McCormick's jewellery. Everything has been recovered—except her emerald ring."

"You are mad!" Laura's face was ashy white. She pushed by me, opened the door and swept out.

I stood there all alone in the Goodwins' front hall. I didn't know what to do. If Mr. and Mrs. Goodwin had been at home, I might have gone to them immediately with my warning, even though Mr. McCormick had instructed me to leave that to him.

I left the house, carefully closing the door behind me. Labelle's ears pricked forward as I walked up to her. I rubbed her nose. "Labelle, what am I to do now?" She gave a snort, as if she knew exactly what needed to be done. When I thought about it, so did I. Instead of waiting for Laura's grandparents to come home, I must find the local magistrate. He wasn't just a judge. He also performed marriages. Laura had told me that she would soon be Peter Dash's wife. How soon?

William McCormick had assured me that he would write to the magistrate. But what if his message had not yet arrived? Then it was up to me to stop that marriage from taking place. Mr. McCormick also planned to send a message to the Chief Constable to advise him to assign a constable to the case. The constable could arrest Dash and put him in jail. But stopping the marriage came first.

I had to think what Laura would do next, after rushing out of the house. She had been ready to go out. Where was she planning to go? That little white lace veil on her head didn't look as though she were just going for a walk.

I looked both ways up and down the road. Laura was already out of sight. The Goodwins' house was a short distance outside Fort Erie. Maybe she had gone into town. If she was on her way to meet Peter Dash, would she tell him about me and about the things I told her? She might not—if she thought my charges were insane nonsense. But if she did tell him, what would he do?

As fast as I could, I unhitched Labelle, mounted, and galloped into town. I had to find the magistrate. I didn't know where to start looking. A good place to ask directions in any town is the general store, so that was where I stopped. The store was crowded. I waited my turn while a man haggled over a pair of boots that he wanted but considered overpriced. Then there was a woman who could not choose between flowered and striped calico for a dress. There were still a dozen customers in the store when at last I reached the counter.

"Sir, where will I find the Fort Erie Magistrate?" I asked the storekeeper.

"Well, that depends on your business with him."

"I want to stop a wedding."

The storekeeper laughed. "Ho! Ho!" The customers guffawed. I felt my face turning red.

When the laughter had calmed down to a few snickers, the storekeeper took pity on me. "You might find him at his house. It's just up Jarvis Street, by the Court House. I'm sorry I laughed. It was just that the way you said it sounded funny."

"It isn't funny." I rushed from the store. On horseback, it didn't take more than two minutes to reach the house. It was a square, limestone building that looked like a small fortress. As soon as I had tied Labelle to the hitching post, I rushed to the door, seized the brass knocker, and pounded. A woman wearing a white apron over her black dress opened the door.

"I must see the magistrate," I said. "Is he at home?" Not waiting for an answer or an invitation, I brushed past her and stepped inside.

"Mr. Ritchie can't see you now. He has a visitor." Her eyes turned toward a closed door.

"My business is urgent. Tell him that Leonard Goodwin's granddaughter is in danger." I didn't say what the danger was. I just took for granted that the Goodwin name carried weight in Fort Erie.

"I'll ask him," she said stiffly, "if he will see you."

She opened the closed door. Beyond her I saw two gentlemen standing in front of the fireplace talking with each other. At the sound of the door opening, they turned and looked at me. The one gentleman was stout, his head bald with a fringe of grey around the sides. He must be the magistrate. I had no doubt about the identity of the other. It was William McCormick.

"What's this!" exclaimed the magistrate, visibly annoyed at the interruption.

But Squire McCormick called me by my name. "Theodore! You've come just in time."

CHAPTER THIRTY-SIX

$\mathcal{S}$quire McCormick introduced me to Magistrate Francis Ritchie, the Justice of the Peace. After telling the Magistrate about the part that I had played in rescuing and restoring the stolen jewellery, he explained to me his presence in this room at this time.

"Theodore, soon after you left my home, I realized that I needed to be present to back up your story. Sending a message to Fort Erie would not suffice. It is important for Laura's situation to be handled discreetly in order to avoid embarrassment for the family. Fortunately, the stagecoach began its first spring run last week. I booked a place on it. I've been travelling for four days. It appears that I've arrived none too soon."

At that moment the clock on the fireplace mantel struck the quarter hour. *Bong!* The time was fifteen minutes before two.

"Indeed, you have!" Magistrate Ritchie glanced at the clock. "It's time for me to ready myself for either role that I must play—minister or magistrate." He walked across the room to a desk that stood against the wall, opened a drawer, and took out a folded piece of green silk. "My sash," he explained as he unfolded it. "It's the insignia of my office. I wear it whenever I perform any official duty." He draped it over his right shoulder and across his chest, then pinned it at his waist on the left side. "The betrothed couple have made an appointment for two o'clock. I am now prepared to sentence the man either to matrimony or to prison." He smiled grimly at his joke. "Actually, I won't be doing either today. I'm certainly not going to marry them! As for the alternative, the Chief Constable has two constables stationed outside, right around the corner of the house. If they arrest Mr. Dash, it will be tomorrow before they bring him before me to face charges. So let's see what happens."

I heard voices in the hall. Laura's solemn and sweet; Peter Dash's deep and urgent, saying to the maid, "We have an appointment to be married."

The maid answered, "Let me take your coats. His Worship is occupied. He will summon you when he is ready to proceed."

The clock struck two. *Bong! Bong!* Magistrate Ritchie looked at Mr. McCormick and me. "Well, I'm ready. I need witnesses. William, you and Theodore can serve that purpose." He stepped across to the door, opened it and called, "Please come in."

Laura and Peter Dash entered the room. The Magistrate closed the door. Dash looked smoothly handsome, with his black moustaches freshly waxed into sharp points and his dark hair sleek with oil. Laura was wearing a pale grey dress with white frills at the top and big puffy sleeves. On her head was the tiny white veil that didn't quite cover her golden curls. On the fourth finger of her left hand gleamed the emerald ring.

They both looked straight at me standing there. Laura gasped, "Oh, no!" On Dash's face was the same look of fear and dismay that I had seen when, wrapped in a blanket at Adam Bruner's house on Pelee Island, he realized that I was going back to gather up the jewellery that had spilled onto the ice. He had lost that chance to become a wealthy man. Now this opportunity—marriage to a rich woman—was about to be snatched from him.

He saw this even before he heard Mr. McCormick's voice announce, "The young lady is wearing my mother's emerald ring."

Laura fainted, collapsing into a heap on the floor. At the same moment, Dash bolted from the room. Mr. McCormick and I knelt, one on each side of the unconscious girl. Outside the window, I heard shouts and sounds of a scuffle. Magistrate

Ritchie looked out the window. "The constables have arrested him," he said. "They'll lock him up in the town jail. Tomorrow morning they'll bring him before me to be charged. Right now, this young lady needs smelling salts. I keep some in my desk drawer. You'd be surprised to learn how often young ladies faint in my office."

The application of smelling salts soon revived Laura. She opened her eyes to find Mr. McCormick holding her left hand, the emerald on her finger gleaming. "Shall I remove the ring?" he asked gently.

Laura looked around groggily. Her fiancé was no longer in the room. "Please take it. I never want to see it again."

Mr. McCormick eased the ring from her limp finger and slipped it onto the little finger of his right hand. "This is the safest way to carry it. I suppose the thief did the same. When he entered my mother's bedroom and saw the jewellery box— either unlocked, or maybe he smashed the lock—and opened it, he must have recognized the emerald ring as the most valuable piece of all her jewellery. To make sure he had it, he pulled it from its slot and put it on his finger."

"Yes," I said. "That explains why one ring slot was empty when I found the jewellery box."

"Don't talk about it," Laura begged. She closed her eyes. "I want to go home."

Magistrate Ritchie cleared his throat. "Ahem! I have another appointment arranged for two-thirty. I don't want to rush you . . ."

Mr. McCormick helped Laura to her feet "Of course we shall leave at once."

"William," said Magistrate Ritchie," I realize you came here by hired conveyance from the stagecoach stop. I'll have my stable man harness my sleigh to take you wherever you wish to go."

"That's very kind. I'm going to Leonard Goodwin's house, and I'm taking his granddaughter with me." He looked at me. "What about you, Theodore?"

"I came on horseback. I'll follow the sleigh to the Goodwins' house." I wasn't eager to face Mr. and Mrs. Goodwin. I owed them an apology for delivering Laura's letter. But I figured I'd redeemed myself by helping to rescue her. They'd surely want to hear what part I'd played in the story.

"Before you leave," Magistrate Ritchie said to me "I must record your full name and place of residence. Your evidence will be needed at Mr. Dash's trial." I told him that my full name was Theodore Henry Dickson, that my father was Charles Dickson, and that our farm was at Queenston Heights.

"That's only twenty-five miles from here," said Ritchie. "Not too far." He picked up a pen from his desk, dipped it in an inkwell, and made a note on a scrap of paper. Then he ushered us out of his office. After telling the maid to convey his instructions to the stable man, he asked us to wait discreetly in the parlour until the sleigh appeared in front of the house. Still wearing his sash of office, he was ready for his next official duty.

Upon reaching the Goodwin's home, I took Labelle to the stable for water, food and rest. When I joined the others in the house, I learned that Laura had gone straight to bed. Mr. and Mrs. Goodwin, Mr. McCormick and I sat down at the dining room table. The maid brought tea, which Mrs. Goodwin poured. The maid left the room, and the door was closed. Mr. McCormick and I told the whole story. I was forgiven for delivering Laura's letter.

"Laura has a way of twisting people around her little finger," said Mr. Goodwin.

"This time," Mrs. Goodwin said, "Laura was the one to be twisted around somebody's finger."

"No harm has been done," said Laura's grandfather, "so long as the story doesn't spread. We can hope that Laura learns a lesson from this experience."

Mrs. Goodwin took a sip of tea and then set down her cup. "Our granddaughter needs to meet some suitable young men. She often speaks of her friends' social life in Toronto. Her best friend from school, a girl of very good family, has invited her to visit. We must arrange for Laura to spend a season in Toronto. She's sixteen years old—old enough to be presented to the Lieutenant Governor as a debutante. She'd love that."

I, too, wondered what the future held for Laura. But I was eager to be on my way. Labelle had been rested for an hour. If we left now, she could be back in her stall in Mr. Kemp's stable before dark.

And then?

CHAPTER THIRTY-SEVEN

We were close to the end of our journey together. Tonight I would take off Labelle's saddle, put her into her stall, and feed and water her for the last time. When talking to others, I called her my horse. She was not my horse. She never would be. I still had ninety dollars left from the reward Mr. McCormick had given me. Even if Mr. Kemp was willing to sell Labelle, ninety dollars was not enough to buy a horse of her quality.

I didn't look forward to my meeting with Mr. Kemp. He'd lied to me about the muskets. I wondered what he'd say about that. I also wondered how much money was coming to me. He had promised to pay me two dollars every week. But would he want to pay me for all the time I was held up along the way? Maybe not. Still, I hoped for something to add to the ninety dollars in my money belt.

A robin skimmed across the road. The first I'd seen this spring. It cheered me for a moment. The sunshine warmed my face. I took off my coonskin hat. Some places there was ice in the ruts, but mostly the road was muck. That didn't stop Labelle from stepping along briskly. She knew she was nearing home. Horses have a good sense of that. She didn't know that she was never going to see me again. I'd spend the night at the tavern in Chippawa. Tomorrow morning I would set out for home on foot, just as I'd left home on foot ten weeks ago.

Slowly the light faded. I'd been wrong in judging the time it would take to cover the distance from Fort Erie. The yellowy-green willows lost their colour. Bushes became dark clumps, and the trees in the woods beyond the bare fields were black shapes against the grey sky.

It was fully dark when we reached Mr. Kemp's tavern in Chippawa. We went straight to the stable. Howard, the man who looked after Mr. Kemp's horses, was ready to leave the stable when I came in leading Labelle. Howard's eyes opened wide.

"Look who's here! Dory Dickson! I never thought I'd see you again or the horse."

"We got held up for a while, but here we are, safe and sound."

"The mare's looking good, apart from the mud on her legs." He reached out to take the rein from me, but then pulled back his hand. "I'll let you take care of her. It's time for my supper." He watched as I put Labelle into her stall, and then he left the stable.

Labelle wasn't paying attention to either of us. She tossed her head and whinnied cheerfully to her friends in the other stalls. It was dispiriting to me to see her so happy when my head was full of gloom. After giving her food and water and a good grooming, I left the stable. Like Labelle, I was hungry after the long ride from Fort Erie. I was tempted to put off reporting to Mr. Kemp and go straight to the kitchen instead. Nancy would find me something to eat. But Mr. Kemp had to come first.

I scraped my boots on the scraper outside the main door before entering. The tavern's public room was welcoming and warm, just as it had been the first time I saw it. A good fire was blazing in the stone fireplace. The room was empty, except for two men who sat by the fire smoking their pipes. One was Sam Kemp. The other was Duncan Fraser. They looked up at me.

Mr. Kemp rose from his chair. "Welcome back. I've been expecting you."

"Here I am at last. I've brought back the horse safe and sound."

"Take a seat and join us."

Duncan Fraser did not rise from his chair. I noticed that he had on his lap a copy of *The Constitution*, William Lyon Mackenzie's newspaper. Duncan's face wore an amused smile, as if he already knew what I was going to say and what Mr. Kemp was going to say, and he looked forward to hearing the conversation.

When I was settled, Mr. Kemp sat down facing me. "A letter from Jacob Fox reached me yesterday. Jacob wrote how those brigands looted Pelee Island."

"It was bad. They took away everything they could carry, even the lamps from the lantern of the lighthouse."

"It won't happen again. When the invaders got back to Sandusky, the authorities arrested them, stripped them of their weapons and told to go home. President Van Buren has laid down the law. He's serious about the Treaty of Neutrality between the United States and Great Britain."

"Now things will be calm along the border," I said.

"I think so." Mr. Kemp took a slow draw on his pipe. "According to the latest news from Toronto, the British government is finally doing something about the mess we're in. They've appointed the Earl of Durham as Governor-in-Chief of British North American, with commissions to investigate the causes of the rebellion. This is going to end the power of the Family Compact in Upper Canada. The way now looks clear to achieve reform without starting a civil war."

"If you didn't want a civil war, why did you send muskets to arm the Patriots?"

"Ah, yes. Jacob Fox's letter explained what happened to those muskets. Just as well they were never used. I suppose I owe you an explanation."

"Yes, Sir. You certainly do." I looked him straight in the eye.

"Well, Mackenzie had asked me to store them on my property. After the burning of *The Caroline* it wasn't safe to keep them here. I knew the Patriot army needed munitions. I thought you'd deliver them to Jacob Fox and come right back here. I didn't expect Jacob to send you over to Pelee Island with them. He shouldn't have done that. He has adult sons he could have sent."

"His adult sons no longer live at home. I'm closer to grown-up than any of his boys still there."

"Jacob wrote that you were shocked to discover it was a load of muskets you were hauling."

"Of course, I was shocked. It thought it was a loom and spinning wheel."

"That's what I wanted you to think."

"Sir, you lied to me. I may be an ignorant farm boy, but I know that supplying arms to the enemy is high treason. Men are hanged for that."

He looked away. "If you'd been caught, your ignorance would have been a strong defence."

"If I'd been caught, I had nothing to prove I didn't know the sled was loaded with muskets."

"Your young innocent face would be proof enough." He shrugged. "It doesn't matter now. That's all behind us. Dory, I promise that your future duties will be limited to chopping wood and tending fires. I'll let go the boy I hired to replace you."

"He can keep the job. I've made up my mind to go back home."

"I understand why you're upset, and I apologize. But when I hired you, you told me that you needed to find work to help your family."

"We can manage." I certainly wasn't going to tell Mr. Kemp about the ninety dollars in my money belt!

"Well, that's up to you. You're welcome to stay here for the night. The new boy has your little room, but you can sleep on the bench in the kitchen."

Duncan Fraser looked up. I thought he was about to offer me the trundle bed in his room.

Instead, he said, "There won't be any Hunters' Lodge meeting in the kitchen to disturb you. We're finished with those. Most members of the Hunters' Lodge consider that we've achieved our most important goals, because they trust Lord Durham to get rid of the Family Compact. The other members, the radicals who want a republic, have fled to the United States. They may try a couple more times to launch an invasion, but essentially, it's all over." Duncan stood up. He crumpled the copy of *The Constitution* that had been on his lap, and he flung it into the fire.

The flames took hold. All three of us stood watching the newspaper burn. "Just like the *Caroline*," Duncan said grimly. "No more Republic of Canada. Well, I'm going back to Scotland. My life's in danger as long as I stay in Canada. If I'm caught, I'll be charged with treason. If I flee to the United States, I'll be deported back here. Right now, in Toronto, the men who led the uprising at Montgomery's Tavern are awaiting trial. Samuel Lount and Peter Matthews are sure to be hanged. Likely the others will be exiled to Van Diemen's land. Neither prospect appeals to me."

"How will you get back to Scotland?" I asked.

"There are plenty of sympathizers who will hide me—friends from the Hunters' Lodges in Upper Canada and from *les Frères Chasseurs* in Lower Canada. I know safe places from here to Halifax. I'll take ship from Halifax."

The flames in the fireplace died down. *The Constitution* was no more. "It's late," said Mr. Kemp. "Dory, you go to the kitchen before Nancy has all the food put away. You're hungry, aren't you? You and I can settle matters between us in the morning."

CHAPTER THIRTY-EIGHT

ancy found me half a cold chicken for my supper. After bringing me a blanket and a pillow, she went off to her own room. I didn't sleep much that night, and it wasn't the hardness of the bench that kept me awake. Thinking about leaving Labelle tugged me one way, and thinking about seeing my family again tugged me the other. I was still half awake in the morning when Nancy returned to the kitchen to start cooking breakfast.

I got up, folded the blanket, and went outdoors to use the outhouse, thinking that I'd go to the stable to say goodbye to Labelle before returning to the kitchen for breakfast. But when I reached the stable door, I saw that Howard was already there. I knew that I'd start crying as soon as I laid my hand on Labelle's mane, and I wouldn't want Howard to see me bawling like a baby. I figured that I'd made my farewell to her the night before, so now I'd just slip away.

I returned to the kitchen. Nancy had porridge ready, pancakes on the griddle and bacon sizzling in her big frying pan. I took some porridge. There was such a big sore lump in my throat that I could hardly swallow a bite. *I'll just leave*, I thought. *I don't need to talk to Mr. Kemp. He knows I'm going home.*

While I was putting on my outer clothes and saying goodbye to Nancy, I completely forgot about my wages. It wasn't until I'd walked a good quarter mile that I remembered Mr. Kemp's remark last night that we would settle matters between us in the morning. He must have meant that we'd talk about the pay that was coming to me. But this thought didn't make me turn back. I kept on walking.

It was a blustery day, the wind at my back. It didn't feel like spring, the way it had the day before. As I trudged along the muddy road, I tried to think about what lay ahead instead of what I'd left behind. I had ninety dollars in my money belt. With ninety dollars we could buy us a pretty good horse, a milk cow, seed for planting and a feeder pig. I'd tell Ma and Pa how I'd earned the reward. I thought about Anna, and about the book she had given me. I hadn't started to read it yet. But tonight I would. I would read it by candlelight in my own bedroom, where I'd have privacy—which I liked very much, even though I'd happily give up privacy to have my two little brothers, Andrew and Alexander, in the room to pester me instead of lying quietly in their graves.

I'd walked about two miles, my mind occupied with such thoughts, when I heard horses coming behind me at a gallop and a voice shouting, "Ho! Dory!" It was Mr. Kemp's voice. I turned around. There he was, on horseback, one arm extended with his hand holding the rein of a second horse galloping at his side. A dark brown horse. Saddled. No rider. Her thick, glossy mane flying in the wind. Labelle!

I stood speechless, not even breathing as the two horses bore down on me. Mr. Kemp brought them both to a halt. His reddish face was redder than ever from the exercise, and his grey eyes were fixed on me. "Well, Dory, what did you mean by sneaking off without settling our account?"

He dismounted, out of breath. I didn't have a word to say. My eyes were fixed on Labelle, who snorted, then stood staring at me, her ears pricked forward, her sides heaving after the two-mile run.

Mr. Kemp caught his breath. "Yesterday evening, I hadn't made up my mind what I owed you. Twenty dollars for ten weeks didn't seem enough. You deserved something extra because of all you'd been through. Then Howard came to my office this morning to tell me how you'd brought back Labelle. He said he'd never seen a horse better cared for, despite the mud on her legs. He said that when you were putting her into her stall last night, you looked as though your heart was breaking. That's what Howard told me. So I said to myself, 'I never intended to pay the boy this much in lieu of wages, but . . .' "

It sounded as though he was giving Labelle to me. I couldn't believe it. I just stood there, dumb as a post.

"Well, what do you say? Do you think she'll do to pull your father's plough?"

Then it hit me that Labelle was mine. I choked up, and I could feel the tears spilling out of my eyes and running down my cheeks. Mr. Kemp must have understood that I'd be embarrassed to have a man see me crying like that. He put the rein into my hand. "I need to get back to the tavern," he said gruffly. "Busy day ahead."

He mounted and rode away. After a minute I threw my arms around Labelle's neck. I dried my tears on her mane. "Labelle," I said to her. "You're coming home with me to meet your new family." So I got myself up into the saddle—the same saddle that George Fox had given me.

The west wind blew away the clouds. The sun shone. By the time I had ridden the last eight miles to Queenston Heights, the blustery morning had changed into a beautiful spring day. When I reached the start of the lane that led from the road up to our farmhouse, I stopped Labelle. I wanted to take a quiet look before making my entrance. Ahead on my right was the family burial plot. The snow on the ground had melted around the four wooden crosses that marked the graves of Pa's parents and my little brothers. Snowdrops poked up their white petals through the withered grass. Beyond the burial plot, at the top of a tall oak tree, a bunch of noisy crows were raising a ruckus amid the bare branches. Still further up the lane, close to the house, stood a big maple that had a swing suspended on ropes from a lower branch, and on the seat was my sister

Susan. She was soaring, her legs pumping as she ascended to the high point of her flight, then swooped and soared again. I watched for a couple of minutes, enjoying the pleasure she took.

Then I put Labelle into a trot, and we continued up the lane.

Over the cawing of the crows, Susan couldn't hear our approach. But suddenly she saw me riding up the lane. Instantly, her legs stopped pumping. The swing slowed in its motion. At the bottom of its arc, before it had come to a standstill, she jumped off the seat, spilling herself with a shriek into the mud.

In an instant, I was off the horse and pulling her out and up into my arms. She hugged me so tight around the neck that I couldn't breathe. Then Ma, hearing Susan shriek, came running out of the house to see what had happened. So I had Ma hugging me too. Then Pa appeared, coming from the barn. He just stood back, looking at me and then at Labelle and then back at me. When Susan and Ma had finished their hugging, he wiped his hands on his trouser legs, stepped up and shook my hand, man to man. "Welcome back." He took another, closer look at Labelle. "That's a mighty fine horse." I could see that he was waiting for an explanation.

"I've been working for Mr. Kemp, the owner of the tavern in Chippawa. He gave me this mare as my pay. Her name's Labelle. She's ten years old. She's a Canadian horse."

"None finer." Pa scratched his head. "How could a boy like you earn a horse like this?"

When Ma heard me say that I'd been working in Chippawa, she put her hands on her hips and said, "You mean you've been working in Chippawa, just ten miles from home; for nearly three months, and in all that time you never paid us a visit!"

"Easy!" said Pa. "Dory will tell us about it if we give him a chance. Let's go into the house and you can make us a cup of tea."

"First, I'll take Labelle to the barn and put her in old Prince's stall. When I've looked after her, I'll join you in the house." I patted Susan's head. "You can come to the barn with me. Do you want to ride her there?"

Susan nodded her head furiously up and down, "Yes! Yes!"
I gave her a boost onto the saddle. Her feet didn't reach the
stirrups. I led Labelle right up to the barn door and then lifted
Susan off. She came into the barn with me and sat on a heap
of straw while I fed Labelle, rubbed her down and cleaned the
road mud from her hooves.

Susan gripped my hand as we walked to the house. Ma had
the tea ready, as well as a plate of sliced bread. No butter. With
no cow and no money, they couldn't have butter. It made me
feel guilty to think how well I'd been eating, most places I'd
stayed along the Talbot Road. But the teapot and the plate of
bread weren't all that I saw in the kitchen. There was our copper
bath tub, usually dragged out only on Saturday nights. It was
steaming with hot water, and Ma had another kettleful heat-
ing on the woodstove. I laughed. While hugging me, Ma must
have noticed something off-putting about the way I smelled.
That was like her—very particular about keeping clean.

I'd been wondering how to go about announcing the ninety
dollars in my money belt. Now the right opportunity presented
itself. I waited until the tea was finished and the tub filled before
standing up and taking off my shirt. They saw the money belt
around my waist, but I'm not sure they knew what it was until
I had it spread on the kitchen table and started to pull those
banknotes from its pocket. I'd expected that my parents would
be smiling and laughing to see all that money. Instead, they
looked just plain scared.

Ma said, "Dory, this is too much for us to take in all at once—
first, the fine horse and now, all this money."

"I'll start at the beginning," I said. So that's what I did, sitting in the bathtub while Ma scrubbed my back. I started with
my reaching Chippawa the same day I'd left home. When the
water in the tub got cold, I took a break from my story to dry
off and dress into the clean clothes Ma brought me. Then I went
on with my story. Ma and Pa let me tell it as it happened, now
and then exchanging a surprised look. Late in the afternoon,
when I'd reached the part where the sled had broken through

the ice and I was warming up at George Fox's farm on Pelee Island, Ma pushed her chair back from the table and stood up.

"It's time for me to start supper. We have a few potatoes we were saving to use as seed potatoes. I'll cook them up tonight for a treat to celebrate your coming home."

She set to work trimming the potatoes, which were soft and wrinkled, with long pale shoots that she trimmed off and eyes she dug out before putting what was left into the cooking pot. Ma said she felt guilty not having something better to celebrate my coming home.

I said, "Just to be here eating potatoes with you and Pa and Susan is all the celebration I need."

All through supper and late into the evening I kept talking. Pa's eyes narrowed and his brow was knitted as he listened; I knew he was thinking hard. Susan sat there blinking, holding her rag doll on her lap, and trying to stay awake so she wouldn't miss anything. It was about nine o'clock, way past her bedtime, before I finished and Ma took her away to put her to bed.

While Ma was out of the room, Pa said. "I've been thinking that if we can pull those stumps out of the back field, we'll be able to plough and plant in straight lines. That will double what we can grow in that field."

"We'll do that," I said. "Labelle can pull stumps just as well as she can haul a sled. What do you aim to plant in the back field?"

"Maybe corn. What do you think?"

"Corn sounds good." I was pleased that he asked my opinion.

"Son, you came back just in time."

I could see how true this was. Just in time for spring planting. Just in time to save the farm. "I was thinking we ought to buy a milk cow, if you know where we can get a good one."

"I believe I do."

Ma came back to the kitchen. She didn't sit down. "I have your room ready for you, Dory. There's clean sheets, a quilt I finished making while you were away, and a fresh nightshirt."

I told her I'd be ready to go to bed as soon as I'd checked on my horse. Pa gave me a lantern to light my way to the barn.

When I'd made sure Labelle was happy in her stall, I returned to the house. I took a lighted candle to my room, along with my saddlebag, which I laid on the blanket box at the foot of my bed. The only thing I took from the saddlebag was the book that Anna Fox had given me. *Lamb's Tales from Shakespeare.* After undressing and putting on the clean nightshirt, I sat on the side of my bed to read for a while. "The Tempest" was Anna's favourite story. I'd told her I'd read it first. Then I'd write a letter to Anna. In my mind's eye I saw her sitting at the little table in the sitting room of Jacob Fox's house, her light brown hair braided smoothly and her thoughtful eyes cast down as she read my letter. Maybe, after she finished reading it, Anna would write a letter to me.

Acknowledgments

In my research for *Battle on the Ice* I have received valuable assistance from individuals, institutions and organizations from Fort Erie to Pelee Island. In particular, I thank the Harrow Early Immigrant Research Society (HEIRS) and especially Ted Steele, Rick McCormick and Bill Brundage. I also thank Kim Gardner, Director of the Pelee Island Heritage Centre, for her assistance on several occasions. Others who have helped me include Archives Volunteer Jack Hodge of the Diocese of Huron Archives and Sean Fleming, Adult Services Librarian, Fort Erie Public Library.

My thanks also to the following persons: Dean G. Taylor, Professor Emeritus Ryerson University, for his knowledge of 1830's firearms; to Alec McCormick for sharing his research into McCormick family history; to my friend and guide Ruth Nicholson UE; to my daughter Alison Baxter Lean for introducing me to the Canadian horse and for her critical acumen in making suggestions to improve the story; to my son John Baxter for providing an extensive bibliography of Resources Related to the Upper Canada Rebellion of 1837; to Anne Haberl Baxter for technical assistance in preparing the final draft for submission; to Millie Czarnik for filling in gaps in my knowledge of the Fox family's history on Pelee Island; and most deeply to my husband and best friend Leigh Smith for his support and encouragement. My final debt of gratitude is to someone no longer with us, the late Ronald B. Hatch, my editor and publisher for twenty years.

There are dozens of histories, journals and memoirs, websites, archival documents and research papers behind the story in

Battle on the Ice. Here are three that I found especially valuable: *Point au Pelee Island,* by Thaddeus Smith; A *Brief History of the Pelee Island Lighthouse,* by Ronald Tiessen and Irene Knezevic; and *The Patriot War,* by Robert Ross, which is archived in the Alpheus Felch Historical Library at the University of Michigan.

In closing, I would like to thank Tina Crossfield of Crossfield Publishing, who was happy to bring this important piece of Canadian history into the light, and Magdalene Carson for her artful and true portrayal of the story on the cover and her creative interior layout.

About the Author

Jean Rae Baxter holds a B.A. and M.A. from the University of Toronto and a B.Ed. from Queen's. She was nominated for the 2022 Governor General's History Award for Popular Media: the Pierre Berton Award.

Although she grew up in Hamilton, "down home" was Essex County, where her ancestors had settled, some as Loyalists in the 1780's following the American Revolution and some a century earlier, in the days of New France.

Jean has written six historical novels, the "Forging a Nation Series," covering the period from 1777 to 1793:

The Way Lies North (2007)
Broken Trail (2011)
Freedom Bound (2012)
The White Oneida (2014)
Hope's Journey (2015)
The Knotted Rope (2021)

With *The Battle on the Ice,* she moves ahead to the Patriot Wars of 1837-1838. Jean's historical novels have won awards in

Canada and the United States, including all three Moonbeam medals --Gold, Silver, Bronze—for Young Adult Historical Fiction.

She has also authored a murder mystery, *Looking for Cardenio*, and two short story collections, *Twist of Malice* and *Scattered Light*.

As a teacher of creative writing Jean holds workshops on using the tools of fiction to bring family history to life.